# THE MOOR

(Books I-III of the Crusader Trilogy)

Reina Donovan

# TABLE OF CONTENTS

# THE MOOR

(Book One)

medical or professional advice. The content of this book has been derived from various sources. Please consult a licensed professional before attempting any techniques outlined in this book.

By reading this document, the reader agrees that under no circumstances are is the author responsible for any losses, direct or indirect, which are incurred as a result of the use of information contained within this document, including, but not limited to, —errors, omissions, or inaccuracies.

# *Introduction*

I t was the dead of night. The cold darkness stole the warmth from the heart of Gabriella. She almost thought of turning back and getting back into her cozy bed. But, she knew her favorite cousin was waiting for her and he was doing this despite not being fully convinced because of her desires.

Gabriella stole through the long verandah of her magnificent mansion looking over her shoulder to see if anyone is there. It was a new moon night and there was nothing except deathly darkness all around. Her heart was palpitating crazily. She had never thought it would come to this. But, she had no choice. Her parents refused to give in.

She was forced to run! She was not born to live without a bigger purpose than to be a good wife to another rich man (maybe even richer than her parents) and simply bear him children. She was not born to knit and sew and merely entertain other rich guests of her husband's (whoever he maybe). She was not born to die of boredom.

She, Gabriella, was born for greater things. She was born to fight. She was born to kill the plunderers of her beloved Mordo. She was sent to be the princess of Mordo so that she could spare her kingdom from the pains of the Moors who had been plundering it for the last 500 years! She was born to take an active part in the Second Crusades called by His Holiness, the Pope. She was born to kill anyone who dared to slur Christians and Christianity.

But her parents thought differently. They believed a woman's rightful place was next to her husband looking after his home and bearing him children while he went and fought in wars. Her mother tried to convince her of her foolhardy thought and told her that a woman's heart once trapped in a man's heart will never find its way out. Love had the power to control a woman. But love did not have the power to control a man!

And so here she was, in the dead of night when everyone else was sleeping, trying to flee with her cousin from her mother's side, Prince Ralph of Gascoigne, Mordo's neighbor. As promised, her dear cousin Ralph was ready by the riverbank with her favorite mare, Constantine. She quickly climbed on and along with Ralph galloped off into the dead of night.

As she turned and looked at her beautiful home, the Castle of Mordo, she suddenly felt a sense of fear and uncertainty. The round towers seemed to give her some kind of warning. The cross over the chapel appeared to be frowning down upon her. And then she remembered that she wanted to go to the chapel and pray before she left home. She had wanted to ask for forgiveness for causing pain to her parents. But in her hurry, she completely forgot! Now, it was too late to go back. And she was too excited about the adventures that lay ahead of her!

# *Chapter 1*
# HAROUN

Haroun watched Peasant Rafe sauntering down the alleyway after taking one drop too many to drink. He stealthily follows him knowing fully well that his bronzed facial features will not be seen by anyone on the new moon night. Being the efficient killer he was, Haroun chose this night for his deadly deed.

After all, the moonlight can help people recognize him if they do manage to see him commit his crime. Not that the death of Peasant Rafe will stir anyone to action. Yet, Haroun was trained to be efficient and so he was.

As Peasant Rafe sauntered ahead, Haroun picked up speed and very soon caught up with the drunken man. He drew close and tripped him. Catching him as Rafe fell down because of the tripping, Haroun very efficiently slit his throat in one swift motion. Rafe did not even realize that he was dying and it did not even get the time to scream in agony as he was dead

11

almost instantaneously! Slowly dropping the corpse onto the pavement and wiping off the few drops of Rafe's blood on the floor of the pavement, Haroun continued walking as if the kill was a mere inconvenience.

He walked about two miles before he reached the meeting point where he was paid for his deed. He took the money, did not bother to receive or give thanks, and went his way. Haroun was a trained assassin. He killed for money. He did not take any sides based on any other kind of morals except the moral of economy and commerce. He worked for whoever paid him!

Haroun walked into a tavern at the end of the city and bought himself some food. He always avoided ale on the day he committed the crime. He needed his wits around in case something went wrong and he had to escape or fight those who came to take revenge, if ever.

He bit into the bread and drank the hot bone soup. As he was having his dinner, he overheard some casual conversation at another table.

"Where's Rafe tonight?" asked one man.

"Don't know and don't care!" replied another.

"Heard his wife is been whoring around with some big man in the castle and Rafe found out about it and has kept her prisoner in their home?"

"Pity! She was a sight for sore eyes. Big eyes! Big breasts! Would have loved to have her whoring with me," guffawed the other fellow.

Paying no heed to this, Haroun's thoughts, as is wont when he was alone, went back to his childhood. He was born into a rich Moor family which could trace its origins back to Tangiers when his grandfather thrice or four times removed came to Andalusia in an effort to spread Islam.

The Moors became so powerful and widespread that at one point in time, their kingdom extended to the Pyrenees to the far north of the Iberian Peninsula. Haroun's family moved from strength to strength and become one of the closest families to the Muslim royal family. The future generations of Haroun's family continued to flourish in Medieval Spain as they learned to blend with the local community as much as possible although they kept their religion and rituals as true to the original as possible. Yet the Moors were treated with respectful fear as their temper and viciousness and passion for remorseless violence were famed all over Andalusia.

Although his ancestors made a lot of wealth and lived a life of luxury, when Haroun was born, his family was on its downward slide and riches and wealth were only spoken of as history. His father wasted his life drinking away the last of the family money and lived merely on past glory. There was little love for his father, Haroun thought to himself. "May his soul rot in hell!"

Now, Haroun's mother Ariana was his mentor! She came from an illustrious Moor family too and was very proud of her ancestry. She taught Haroun warring and fighting skills. She always said, "Remember you are a Moor! A powerful and strong Moor! Born to rule! Never bow your head to anyone but the Lord above!"

When his father passed away, Haroun actually heaved a sigh of relief. He was happy that there would be no more beatings and curses to take from the vile man. But, unluckily for Haroun, his mother followed her husband sooner than both of them would have liked and Haroun was an orphan at the tender age of ten!

There were numerous uncles and aunts and

cousins in the large, rambling, and dilapidated family castle that was held up only because of pity from God above (as He did not want to wipe out an entire Moor family at once). At least this is what Haroun thought as the walls became unbearably damp during the winters and rainy season and the number of gaping holes in the roof allowed for more water to fall inside the castle than outside when it rained heavily.

He left home a week after his mother passed away. He told himself, "There is nothing for me there now!"

He took shelter in a tavern on the outskirts of the city. He lived here doing odd jobs for the tavern owner in return for food and accommodation. Food was in the form of leftovers and accommodation was under the tables after the tavern closed for the day. His day began at the crack of dawn and he worked till his feet fell sore till past midnight curling up under one of the tables when the tavern doors closed. Yet, he did not complain because he loved this sense of new-found independence.

One day, two hefty men walked into the tavern and placed their orders for alcohol.

"Two large!" cried one and the other pushed and

shoved a man sitting quietly with his drink at a nearby table and forcibly sat down at the now empty table. The fallen man picked himself up and walked away without a comment although Haroun did notice a gleam of something in his eyes. The partner guffawed at this scene and sat down heavily on a chair too next to his friend.

The tavern owner's daughter served them the drinks while they leered at her. She was used to this and hence she ignored them and started walking away after filling their cups. But, they started needling her. She yelled at them with some chaste obscenities. This angered them and one of them came lunging toward the girl. Just when everyone present thought the girl was going to get badly hurt, the big man fell down with blood oozing around his throat. He was so fast that no one even saw the quiet man who had walked away earlier, come right in time to slash the throat of the leerer!

People only saw the result; the big hefty man lying slumped down, quite dead, and the quiet man standing over the corpse, his eyes quite remorseless. There was deathly silence all around and only Haroun seemed to have noticed the partner lunge forward ready with belligerent rage to attack the killer with a deadly knife!

"Look out!" Haroun screamed. That day, Haroun's life took a turn as he saved the quiet man's life. Because, even before he screamed, he took one of the serrated hunting knives hanging on the wall of the tavern and drove it right through the big man's heart. Haroun was lucky that his hand reached right at the center of the big bully's heart. He had no time to react as his heart stopped beating immediately. The scream escaped Haroun an instant after he lunged forward! Now, the other partner lay as dead as the first man!

The quiet man walked out of the tavern as if this kill was a mere inconvenience! Haroun stared after him and as he walked out the door, he beckoned to the boy! Haroun walked toward him mesmerized by the entire scene, his little yet powerful hands bloodied with the blood of a man he just killed. The quiet killer held Haroun's hand and led him out! They walked over to a stream that flowed nearby. He helped Haroun wash off the blood from his hands.

"You have skills! Do you want to use them and see the world?"

Haroun dumbly nodded. "Follow me," he said. That was the last Haroun saw of the tavern which was his home for nearly a year!

The following two years was spent in the company of the quiet killer whose name was Sancho. He was part of a gang of pirates. He became a father figure to Haroun, something his original father was never able to be.

He taught Haroun his skill and trade which was that of an assassin. The Moor learned the different ways to kill, how to use the different kinds of knives. He learned to kill by stealth. He learned to kill openly. He learned that killing others allowed him to live and live well. He learned to sail from the pirate gang and he learned to read and interpret the ways of the seas! Haroun and his pirate gang plundered and looted and killed and made more money than he had dreamed of.

The fame of Haroun's skill spread far and wide and people who killed for money efficiently seemed to be in short supply. Work never ceased! The little boy who was now a strapping and powerful young man traveled across Andalusia doing his job as efficiently as possible and with each kill, he gained more wealth.

Now, this was a time in Andalusia when Christian uprising swelled against the Moors. Haroun's skill was needed both by the Moors and the Christians and he took no sides except the side of money. Haroun worked for whoever paid him more. So, sometimes, he was a soldier in the Christian army against the Moors and, sometimes, he was in the army of the Moors against the Christians.

He also worked for people who hired him to take care of troublesome people in their lives. That was the job he just accomplished by killing Peasant Rafe. He never asked for reasons why someone wanted to kill someone else. If he got paid, he killed. He was a popular killer as his ability to use his skills was matched by no one in the whole of Andalusia! Yet, h had to be careful because the victims' family could be searching for him to take revenge. And Haroun had definitely had made far more than his share of enemies.

# *Chapter 2*
# GABRIELLA

Gabriella was the beloved daughter of Lord Esmour Martyn of Mordo. Being the only child and surrounded by a male cousins, Lord Esmour lavished love and affection on her. Gabriella's mother, Lady Irene, was the daughter of the highly respected and illustrious king of Galuven descended from one of the Templar Knights going back many generations. Gabriella was brought up in luxury as should be a princess of high standing.

She was highly influenced by the Catholic Church to which both her parents belonged. However, her royalty combined with a strict Catholic upbringing did little to stymie Gabriella's rebellious streak. While she was a devout Catholic she was very headstrong and believed in feminine power. She openly criticized many of the customs of her times which made women subjugated under a man.

"Why should I be under the thumb of anyone?" she asked of her mother. Her fiery eyes lit up her beautiful face and the blueness in her eyes seemed swallowed by the golden fire that they emanated when she felt slighted by such formalities. Gabriella insisted on learning all the things her male cousins and brothers learned.

She took fencing, sword-fighting, and horse-riding lessons. And she was so good at them that in the many duels that she had with her cousins, she came out easily victorious. Her favorite cousin was Ralph who was her constant companion and was very understanding of her rebellious nature. In fact, he encouraged her to be independent and taught her a lot more skills of a warrior than was allowed for a woman in those days.

While Lord Esmour adored his daughter blindly, Gabriella's mother was stricter with her. She admonished her for her brazenness and warned her of consequences that she will not be able to bear if she chose to rebel to such an extent. She tried to teach Gabriella knitting and sewing. But the stubborn girl refused to learn.

Her refusal had nothing to do with her incapability but a lot of do with the fact that activities like knitting and sewing were lady-like and she did not want to be anything lady-like. She really abhorred being told to do anything against her will.

Yet, Gabriella was a devoted Catholic and attended Bible classes regularly. In these classes, she learned about the Crusades and the stories of brave knights and warriors fighting to keep her religion free from foreign invaders and influences drove her deep desire to be part of the Crusades.

But her mother would hear none of it. And in this regard, her doting father supported her mother wholeheartedly.

"I can't live at home in peace knowing that my dear daughter is facing dangers in the war. Anyway, those hardships are for men. You just look pretty and have a rich life filled with luxuries. Have plenty of children and shower them with love like how your mother does and how her mother did before her! I only gave in to your whim of wanting to learn to fight so that you can save yourself if in a quandary! Not to run off to fight the Crusades!" he said.

Deeply disappointed by the turn of events, Gabriella hatched a plan. She had heard of Captain Philip who was in Mordo recruiting knights for the Crusades. She was going to join his army whether her parents gave her permission or not!

However, Gabriella was smart enough to know that she will need help and who else could she turn to but her trusted cousin, Ralph?

"You are completely mad!" This was Ralph's initial reaction at her running off idea. But slowly Gabriella convinced him of her strength of resolve in this matter and that she was not doing this because she wanted to prove something but because it was a calling. She was born into this family so that she could fight for its safe upkeep. Otherwise, she would not have felt this deep urge to do leave her loving parents, especially her doting father, and run off into unknown dangers. Ralph was convinced a little. But his love for his cousin was the bigger reason he was willing to take the risk. Gabriella understood this.

So, the day when the two cousins planned to run dawned bright and clear. Captain Philip was stationed about 50 miles away from Mordo and she needed about two to three days to reach him. She surreptitiously packed food and clothing for her journey. Ralph was to meet her at the riverbank with her mare, Constantine and they were both going to flee.

Things went according to plan and the day after their escape, the two royals were about 25 miles away from Mordo. They were in the middle of a lush green forest the beauty of it only being broken by occasional sounds of wild beasts. Sometimes, Gabriella thought she heard the growling sounds of bears. Despite being a strong person who is not easily scared, the Princess of Mordo did find her hair standing on edge at these wild sounds coming from different parts of the thick dense forests.

The two of them stopped only for meals and to wash themselves of grime and dirt. During the night, Ralph pitched tents he had brought. Ralph spoke very little during the journey and Gabriella attributed this to his sense of fear and uncertainty which were the emotions that she was going through as well. So, she too stayed to herself, kept her thoughts to herself, and spoke very little. Yet, Ralph was more nervous than was necessary, she thought.

After all, the plan was perfect. Ralph had pretended to leave for his castle about two days before and he had stayed with an uncle unknown to everyone else. He wanted to return to his kingdom as he was not as keen as her to join the Crusades. So, they plotted a plan where he will help Gabriella and yet be able to return home.

Everyone at Mordo thought Ralph was in Gascoigne and he had people there who would verify his story including the uncle who lived in Mordo and had a home in Gascoigne as well. After ensuring that Gabriella was safely ensconced with Captain Philip, Ralph would return home and pretend surprise at the absence of Gabriella. She thought it was a foolproof plan and they had worked out the details quite so that there would not be a problem for him. Still, why was he so worried?

"Ralph, I am sorry I dragged you into this. But can you please relax now that things are going fine." Gabriella said before retiring to her tent the second night. He just scowled at her and this really did surprise her. Ralph had never scowled at her before. He must be worried about something.

She was too headstrong a woman to allow someone else to take undue discomfort for her sake. So, she told him, "Listen Ralph. I completely understand the anger you are feeling toward me. I am truly grateful for what you have done for me till now. I think I will be able to manage from here. Why don't you return to Gascoigne as planned from here itself?"

Ralph looked at her mysteriously and his eyes gleamed. But he said nothing. He just turned and went into his tent and pulled down the flap shutting her out of his world. Gabriella was amazed how someone whom she trusted and cared for and who trusted and cared for her in equal measure could suddenly become a stranger? Maybe, it was the effects of the strange jungle.

She went to bed with a heavy heart not sure at all if she can manage without Ralph. But, she was certain about her next step. She would get up before dawn and go away without Ralph. "I am being too much of a burden on him and I don't think it's fair!"

She lay down on her mattress made of leaves and thought of her luxurious bed at home. Strangely she did not miss the luxury. But, she did miss the attention and love that she was showered with at home. She lay back and thought of her beautiful castle at Mordo.

# *Chapter 3*
## THE CASTLE OF MORDO

While Gabriella spent her first night outside of the Castle of Mordo, she couldn't help remembering each detail of the stupendous structure that was her home. She knew every nook and corner of the castle and she had walked the myriad underground maze of tunnels and dungeons a thousand times. She enjoyed every trip with her father into the maze and she came away astounded by the labyrinthine tunnels. She became so well-versed with them that she could hide for days on end without being found except if she wanted to be found!

Her mind raced through the various parts of the castle which was her home until yesterday. She knew that she would go back to it victorious in her efforts to slay the marauders invaders. But for now, it remained only in her thoughts.

Her thoughts traced the innumerable arrow loops found across the outer walls which were built to shoot arrows at the oncoming enemy army while remaining safe within the walls of the castle. She could almost feel the smoothness of the Ashlar blocks that were used to build the entire rambling castle.

In her mind, she ran through the 25 different baileys spread across the castle surrounded by walls that kept the inmates safe. There were baileys in the upper deck, in the lower deck, on the east side, and on the west side. These baileys were the favorite playgrounds for her and her cousins. She would undergo her fencing, sword-fighting, and horse-riding trainings here.

She thought of the stately barbican that housed the guards who kept watch over the gates of the castle. She had stayed with old Stephen in the barbican many times when he stood guard and told her innumerable battle stories. She remembered the hundreds of times she raced with her cousins all around the barmkin. Invariably, she was one of the very few who did not get breathless even when she ran around the barmkin hundreds of times.

She remembered the number of times she climbed up till the bartizan and the bastion to get a bird's eye view of entire Mordo. She loved to look at her kingdom from this height. How many times she had pictured herself ensconced in one of the battlements in imaginary battles that she fought with an oncoming Moor army.

One of her favorite haunts of Castle Mordo was the large courtyard where she played, trained, and spent a lot of happy times with her cousins. She loved to look at the drawbridge each time it was raised or lowered and whenever she heard the sound of its movement, she would run across to the vantage point to watch the drawbridge being lowered and raised. She loved listening to the sounds the drawbridge as the guards used the lever mechanism to pull it up or lower it down.

Gabriella loved leaning over the embrasures and many times her father had come running to her scared that if she leaned too much over then she could slip over the wall! She loved to scare him like this and always used this trick to get him to come to her and give her one of his warm hugs. The hallway was one of her favorites too. She loved the chandeliers hanging all over and always helped the servant light them up whenever she could. She loved the way the servants pulled the rope once all the candles were light and her eyes gleamed as she saw the lit-up chandelier rise up to the roof!

Another favorite place was the moat. She enjoyed the swishing of the water in the moat and she loved to feed the huge crocodiles there. She knew no one dared enter the castle by trying to swim through the moat. The crocodiles were lying in wait to have such people for their supper. The depth of the moat was also capable of sending shivers down the spines of the best swimmers.

Although during her lifetime, the murder hole was never used, she had heard lots of stories from old Stephen while she talked with him in the barbican. Huge balls of fire would be thrown through these murder holes to kill incoming besiegers. The Castle of Mordo was highly protected.

Gabriella loved to look through the trelliswork of the oriel windows spread all across the castle. She would press her face on the trelliswork and feel the designs being etched onto her skin. She cherished that feel. She had once tried to take a peek into the oubliette to see the prisoners who were held captive there. But, her father took this very seriously and he refused to talk to her till she promised that she would never try to do this again. And Gabriella has stuck to her promise. She never tried to get into the oubliette.

She cherished those moments in the castle when she and Ralph would quietly sneak out through the postern to spend some time in the thick jungle behind and splashed in the cool waters of a spring nearby. She remembered once trying to push open the Yett and finding it impossible for it to move even by a hair's breath. It needed the strength of four elephants to push open the Yett when needed.

Her world revolved around the Castle of Mordo. She knew of no other world except that of Mordo. And yet, the heroic stories of the Crusaders filled her with a desire to see and take part in the Crusades. As these thoughts flew past her head, she got drowsy and fell asleep into a dream of Crusades and knights and warriors. Her soft mattress at home was replaced by uncomfortable leaves and bark. And yet, she felt a strange sense of anticipation. Like her life was going to change drastically.

"I have to be ready to sacrifice if I choose to work for Him," she thought and fell asleep.

She was dreaming that she was fighting in the Crusades and Captain Philip was very happy. She was fencing with enemy warriors and chasing them out of her precious land. She was staring into the dark eyes of the most handsome man she had ever seen and suddenly she realized that the last thing was not a dream.

There was this handsome man with rippling muscles and intense dark eyes staring into her. She stared back with wonder for a long time before she realized that a serrated knife fell off from his right hand and nearly struck her leg. She jumped up and screamed. The man simply let go of her and only then she realized that she was cradled in his arms and their faces were as close to each other as was possible for two human faces to be!

# *Chapter 4*
# THE MEETING

fter he dropped her, Gabriella lay on her makeshift mattress for a little while completely mesmerized by the face that was looking down on her. She then spotted the knife and gingerly picked it up. It was a thing of beauty. Its dark-brown wooden handle was carved beautifully and the serrated edges were really sharp.

She just touched it and immediately drew her hand back as it seared her skin and a drop of blood oozed out. She was too amazed at the turn of events. She got up and went outside the tent. There was no sign of the man. Who was he? Why was he in her tent? Was he a tribal who was looking to rob? Strangely, she felt no fear! She only felt a peculiar kind of warmth in her heart that was completely new to her!

Calling out for Ralph, she approached his tent and peered in. He was not there. Did he flee after the intruder? Anyway, she thought that this intruder episode suited her plans well. It was time for her to move on without Ralph. She hoped to reach Captain Philip's army by evening and so she abandoned her tent and simply left with a small satchel of food and her water bag.

She climbed onto her Constantine and prodded her on towards Captain Philip. She would have traveled for about an hour and a part of her heart wanted to see Ralph coming for her. Another part wanted to see that handsome face again. She thought she had forgotten about the intruder but his dark intense eyes refused to leave her thoughts. She felt that some part of her was left behind in those eyes.

"Who was the man? And why do I feel so strange about him? After all, he seemed to have come to either rob or, perhaps, even rape her? Then why did she not feel anger or resentment against him? What thoughts were running behind those intense eyes that seemed to probe deep into her soul?" These uncomfortable thoughts raced through her mind as she rode towards Captain Philip and his Crusading Army.

As she moved ahead, she continued to hear the sounds of various wild animals and despite her sense of confidence, she was scared. But, she refused to give in to her fears and galloped on.

Suddenly, through the trees, came three masked men who pounced on Gabriella dropping her off her horse. She was shaken only for a moment. She immediately jumped on to her feet and took out her sword and started fighting the bandits off. The men were quite surprised to see such agility in a woman and they did not expect this at all. One of three men fell down wounded badly.

The other two lunged forward together and Gabriella knew that she would not be able to handle them on her own. She now thought of her parents and said to herself, "Maybe this is the end!" But, she will not go down without a fight. She fought valiantly but the men were not bandits without training. Both struck together and her sword flew from her hands and fell some distance away. She quickly took out her small knife and struck one of the two men on his thigh. He screamed in pain. But, the agony only angered him further and with the help of his partner pinned Gabriella down on the ground.

The men leered as they began tearing bits and pieces of her clothing. She felt quite helpless. But she knew this was not how she wanted her life to end. She wanted to die fighting in the Crusades not raped by bandits in the forest!

At this point in time, out of the blue, two arrows came in such rapid succession that the two men fell over each other in a heap without even realizing what hit them. The arrowheads had pierced the center of their hearts!

Gabriella got up and hastily arranged her clothing and looked in the direction from where the arrows came. She found the same pair of intense dark eyes staring back at her! She gasped as she watched the man come out from his hiding place and walk towards her! The muscles in his hands and legs were rippling with energy and his demeanor made it appear that he did everything with incredible ease.

He walked towards Gabriella and she continued to stare at him completely under his spell. He too seemed to be in some kind of spell as he moved towards her. When they were close enough, he simply bent down and kissed her full on her lips and she too simply responded to the thrill of his kiss. She kissed him back and when they drew away from each other after a while, they were both breathless.

"Who are you?" she managed to ask. He did not respond. Instead, he lifted her and put her on her horse and told her, "I will come with you till Captain Philip's army where you will be safe from raping marauders!"

They rode together for some time and he picked juicy fruits for her! He watched her while she ate and simply did not understand what he felt for her. He had had many women and never had he felt for anyone the way he was feeling for Gabriella.

She was supposed to be his next kill. Her cousin, Ralph, had paid him a substantial amount to kill her. Ralph had told him of her plans to join the Crusades. He had pre-planned the route they were going to take and told him to waylay her on the way and slit her throat. As was his norm, Haroun did not bother to find out the reason. He only made sure that Ralph made the advance payment and had followed both of them from the outskirts of Mordo.

As he followed them waiting for her to get into a relaxed state before attacking, he found her ways very intriguing. Here was a rich woman who could have anything she wanted and yet, she was running away to fight the Crusades!! Wow, how many women happily exchange places with her? And she was going n the reverse direction!

"Anyway, what do I care? I will do my job and

then move on to the next," he had told himself as he followed her and watched her from a distance.

Then, on the second night of the journey, when she had settled in to her tent, Ralph and he met and decided that now the time was ripe. Ralph left for his home knowing well that there is no way Haroun is going to miss his victim. He has never missed any victim till now! So, why would he miss killing Gabriella? Ralph decided not to wait for the macabre event to actually take place and see the dead body of his cousin. He just decided to go home to give his uncle the good news.

Haroun stealthily crept into Gabriella's tent, his serrated knife ready in his right hand. He looked down at Gabriella and suddenly, something clicked. He looked into that beautiful face and he knew he would never be the same again. All his training was a complete waste. He could not bring himself to lift his right hand and slit her throat. Instead, he put his left hand under her neck and gently lifted her face. He wanted to kiss her! At that moment, she opened her eyes and they were the most brilliant blue he had ever seen! He felt his heart lurch and the knife fall from his hand.

He knew he had fallen in love at that moment. He knew that he would do everything in his power to keep his love safe. The only thing he felt saddened about at that time was the fact that it is most unlikely that she will love him back.

Then, suddenly today, when this event with bandits happened. He had been following her since she left the tent after finding Ralph's tent empty. He followed her this time not to kill but to keep her safe. The wild animals were not as much a problem as bandits, he knew.

Haroun knew of the deadly Three Killers gang was somewhere in the vicinity. He realized that they must have, by now, seen the young beautiful princess wandering the forest alone. They will not let go of such an easy prey. To save her from bandits is why he chose to follow Gabriella.

And they came and lunged at her. Haroun was about to rush to her aid when he saw with what amazing agility Gabriella got onto her feet and wounded one of three men! He watched her move with speed and accuracy swishing her sword and attacking her attackers fearlessly. Haroun had never met a woman like her! Now, he was truly and irretrievably in love with

Gabriella.

Despite her attempts, the two remaining men were onto her like animals. At that point, he let go of two arrows that pierced their hearts like in the center. Then, he watched her blue eyes scan the area and rest on him. Now, he was truly overcome. He walked out of his hiding place and went to her and kissed her.

To his surprise, she kissed him back with passion! He was bewitched beyond reason. Was she smitten too? "Oh, I wish the pain in my heart stopped and I knew for sure she was in love with me as much as I was!"

They broke away and were breathlessly looked at each other. Then, getting his wits back, Haroun lifted her and put her on her horse. She asked him who he was. He couldn't bring himself to answer her and instead told her that he will accompany her till she reached the safety of Captain Philip.

# *Chapter 5*
# CHANGE OF PLAN

A round noon, while taking a break from the journey under the shade of a large old tree, Gabriella asked the man (she still did not know his name and she had already kissed him!), "So, what were you doing in my tent? Same thing as the bandit? To ravish me?"

Haroun looked at her and then away. He couldn't meet her eyes because, for the first time in his entire life, he wanted to be someone other than what he was. He wanted to tell Gabriella that he was a builder or a carpenter or a farmer! Anything but a killer! It was indeed strange that he was ashamed to show his true colors to her! Is this what love is? To hide the wrongs and show only the nice thing!

Something stirred within him and he decided to lay bare his life to Gabriella. He started, "My name is Haroun and I am a sword for hire! I kill for money. And this is what I have been doing the past 15 years of my life. Killing for a living!"

Gabriella's blue eyes went bluer and she started

41

from her place and ran helter-skelter. He stayed where he was and made no attempt to pursue her. Gabriella climbed onto her horse and rode away as far as she could from the man she was hopelessly falling in love with! He was a murderer, a killer? And he was a Moor.

Here she was trying to fight against Christian enemies and today, she had given her heart to a Moor? Her mind was in turmoil. She had reached a stream and got off from her horse. Splashing water over her face, hoping that the nightmare she was living was only a nightmare and she would wake up in her warm bed. When she opened her eyes, Haroun was there in front of her and his dark intense eyes seemed to penetrate her soul again. She was hopelessly in love with him. Despite knowing his roots, she wanted to love him.

She reached out and pulled him to her bosom and they held onto each other's love. Haroun looked up at her and said, "I don't know why Gabriella, but I love you and I know that I want you to be by my side till I die!"

Gabriella's eyes lit up with unshed tears and she told him, "Yes, Haroun, I only know your name and I know you are from the enemy camp. Yet, I love you and I know not why too!"

They kissed, first gently. Slowly the kiss became more passionate and they had to literally tear away from each other lest the passions overtook their sense of dignity in the open jungle.

"So, what were you doing in my tent?"

"I was there to kill you!"

"What? Why? We don't even know each other?"

"I told you I was a killer by profession and someone had paid me to kill you."

Gabriella reeled under the impact of this new knowledge! The only person who was aware that she will be in this jungle on this path was Ralph! So, he must have been involved somehow! Why?

She looked to Haroun for help! He seemed as baffled. "I never ask for the reason. I just follow orders once the payment has been made. Yes, it was Ralph who approached me and paid me to murder you. But I do not know why?"

They both sat in silence. Haroun was feeling miserable for putting Gabriella to so much pain. But, he knew he was right in having confessed himself to her. His heart felt freer and he felt he deserved her love more than before. He did not hide who he was and yet she proclaimed her love. There must be some deeper connection between us. For the moment, Haroun was simply happy to revel in his feeling of mutual love.

Gabriella, on the other hand, was having confusing thoughts. Her trusted Ralph wanting to kill her! Why? She thought back to the wonderful times she had spent with her cousin and not a single time did it strike her that he was feeling so much animosity towards her. What had she done? And, in addition to these confusing thoughts, was the overwhelming love she was feeling for this Moor. Why was she so attracted to him? And what was she to do?

Haroun broke into her thoughts, "If you will listen to me, I think I might help you unravel some amount of confusion from your mind. Let us go back to Mordo. You go to your father and confess your guilt for having run away! Yes, he is going to be really angry. But, that is the only way you will know why Ralph wanted you killed. And I now know you can never live in peace until you have an answer for that!"

Gabriella looked at him in wonder. He can read her mind too! Yes, I will never find peace till I know what made Ralph so angry that he wanted me killed! I have to get to the truth of the matter.

So, they turned back and were on the outskirts of Mordo in two days. Haroun stopped her when they had reached the outskirts and told her that he will not come into Mordo. He was after all a Moor and Mordo was a Christian kingdom and he will not be spared. "I now want to live for this love, my beloved." Gabriella also realized the truth in his statement and she knew that it is quite unlikely that there love has a future. Her parents will never agree to let their only daughter be married to a Moor.

They got off from their horses to say their goodbyes. Gabriella was sobbing openly while Haroun's eyes were filled with unshed tears. They did not kiss but simply hugged each other for some time. Then, he let her go and got onto his horse and rode off back into the jungle.

Gabriella's heart tore to see her beloved's back thinking that this is the last time she will be seeing him. She called out to him silently and he turned back one last time and waved before taking a turn that took him out of her sight.

She rode back to the Mordo castle dejectedly. She knew the space in her chest was empty because her heart had followed Haroun. As she went closer to her home, she found people surrounding her horse and cheering her. Her attempt to join Captain Philip may not have found favor with her parents. But, her people seemed to love her for it. However, they were also curious to know why she returned so early. She promised them that she will give her full story once she reached home and first spoke to her parents.

Word reached the castle before she did and there was a big entourage waiting to receive her joyously. Her father was at the head of the assembly waiting to receive her and he grabbed her in his arms and hugged her shedding copious tears. Her mother hugged her with less fervor and Gabriella knew she was going to have the biggest showdown she had ever had with her mom very soon.

But, that was for later. She looked around for Ralph and did not find him in the crowd. She mentioned nothing about the events in the jungle. She merely told her father that she realized her folly and hence chose to return home. She realized her life's purpose was to serve a Christian knight who will fight in the Crusades while she stayed home and reared his children.

Her father was thrilled to hear about this and immediately announced her marriage to Cousin Ralph. This was not surprising as everyone simply assumed that the friendship between Ralph and Gabriella was more than just platonic and the families of Gascoigne and Mordo were more than happy to see them get married and combine royalty and riches. It would be a perfect political marriage.

Gabriella was taken aback with this announcement. For one, she never felt anything more than a platonic kinship towards Ralph and now this intention of Ralph to get her killed changed even that for her. And, finally, she has given her heart to Haroun and she could not allow anyone to take his place. Yet, she kept quiet hoping to unravel the new mystery around Ralph.

"Where is Ralph?" asked Gabriella.

"Oh! He has gone home to Gascoigne. His parents were here at Mordo in an effort to console your mother. After all, they are her cousins as well! But Ralph is on his way to Mordo."

The betrothal announcement of Gabriella and Ralph called for a celebration and the entire kingdom of Mordo celebrated. The castle rang in the festivities with overflowing wine and feasts. The celebration went late into the night and it was nearly dawn when Gabriella could finally tear herself away from her cousins to speak to her parents.

There was absolutely no sign of Ralph and Gabriella knew exactly why he did not turn up. And she was duty-bound to let her parents know the truth about Ralph.

# *Chapter 6*
# THE TRUTH

---

Gabriella went towards her parent's room and before she could knock on the door, she heard her mother say, "The Moor whore!" Gabriella froze.

Then, she heard the sound of a slap ring through and her father's voice said, "Don't you dare call her that?"

"Of course I will call her by her profession. And to think I was forced to look after her daughter as my own. Disgusting!"

"She is my daughter as well. And if I hadn't found Ayesha, I would have been childless because we have not had a child after that, have we?" This was her father talking!

"Yes, maybe not! But we would not be having a half-Moor for a daughter would we?" her mother screamed. "And I will not let her pollute my family by allowing her to marry Ralph!"

Gabriella could not stop herself and she barged

into the room and watched in horror as flashes of hatred passed between her parents. She had never seen her parents like this before.

"Who is the Moor Whore and who is this daughter you are talking about," demanded Gabriella.

For an instant, her parents just stared dumbly at her. Then, her father's face fell and he watched in dismay as her mother walked across to his beloved daughter and say, "Your mother is the Moor whore and you are the daughter we were talking about!"

Gabriella was too stunned to say anything. She stood rock-still till her mother reached her and shook her! Gabriella saw her father's fallen face and realized that her mother was telling the truth.

She was in a completely dazed state. She flung herself out of the room, ran across the verandah and took the same path that she took a couple of days ago in her bravado attempt to join the Crusades! And here she was today, unsure of her own identity.

She climbed onto the first horse available and galloped away into the night. She drove like a raging woman and she had no idea where she was going! She just let the horse choose his own route.

Soon, she reached the dense thick forest. Completely enervated, she got off from her horse and sat down under a tree on a protruding root. She tried hard to compose her thoughts. She was not her mother's daughter? Her mother was a Moor whore! Why was her Christian father associated with a Moor? Who was she? A Christian or a Moor? She had no answers and her mind was in a web! She just shed copious tears!

Just then, out of the blue, three masked men came at her! Even in her demented state of mind, she realized that one of these was the same bandit she had wounded earlier. Haroun had saved her from the other two. Today, she realized she did not have Haroun to rescue her. But, she refused to die in this humiliating way. So, she sprung forward and quickly took out the dagger from the belts of one of the bandits. She would kill herself before she allowed any of these wretched creatures touch her.

As she was getting ready to either fight or die fighting, she heard a loud roar and out sprang Haroun from the dense thicket with his sword swirling high. The bandits were taken aback but were not ready to give in. A wounded bandit wanted his revenge. Between Haroun and Gabriella, they fought off the bandits again. Haroun was a trained and skilled warrior. If he could kill for money, he could kill twice as fast for love.

He realized this as he swirled his sword all around and wounded the bandits repeatedly. He saw his beloved Gabriella fighting ferociously as well. He felt his heart swell with pride and love for her and he decided at that very moment that no matter who or what came in the way, he will stick to Gabriella till death do them apart. Soon, the bandits were overwhelmed and took off in fright.

Thoroughly exhausted, Gabriella and Haroun fell into each other's arms and held on dearly till their breathing returned to normal. Then, they stepped back and looked at each other with renewed interest. Haroun was astounded that Gabriella was in the jungle again and Gabriella was astounded that Haroun was still around!

Despite their confusing thoughts, they were so happy to see each other! Holding hands, they sat down under the tree and shared their stories that happened in the few hours that they parted. While Gabriella told him her sad story and how she realized in the last few hours that she might not be the person she believed she was, Haroun told her that he couldn't bring himself to go very far away from her. So, he roamed around in the jungle hoping for some kind of miracle.

He looked at her with loving eyes and said, "It seems like my prayer has been answered!"

She smiled back too. But, her mind was still seeking answers and Haroun decided to help her find the answers. They rode back to town and surreptitiously took a place at a local inn for the night. They slept soundly after a harrowing day and felt refreshed the next morning.

Gabriella needed answers. How to get them? She thought it best to approach her father for help. If her mother was not the real one, she knew that her father was indeed the Lord of Mordo. He would provide her with answers.

So, they waited till dark and then went towards the castle. Gabriella knew the ins and outs of the castle and also knew of its many secret passages that her father had shown to her many times. Instinctively, she used one of these passages and reached a door. She pushed and the door opened. She saw her father sitting on the couch and looking toward the door. He knew she will come back and he had kept the door open. By now, word had spread about the infidelity of the Lord of Mordo and how he had raised a Moor child even though he was her father! It was an unforgivable act and the matter was being taken to the Pope for his judgment. Her father will surely be beheaded, she knew! Such a kind of sacrilege had only death written all over it.

She ran toward her father and hugged him. He hugged her back, sat her down beside her and told her, "You deserve to know the story of your mother and my intense love for her." At this point in time, his eyes fell on Haroun. Gabriella immediately said, "I trust him implicitly, my dear father. Otherwise I would not have brought him here."

The Lord of Mordo had a glint in his eye as he studied Haroun. He smiled at his daughter and said, "Strange are the ways of life!"

He then related the story of the lady who was Gabriella's mother. The Lord of Mordo had met her while fighting the Moors. Her husband was killed in a recent battle and the other men of her tribe were fighting over each other to get her. She was disgusted and had run away. The Lord of Mordo had saved her from a pack of wolves and it was love at first sight for him. She took much longer to reciprocate his love but, finally, she did give in.

He brought her secretly to Mordo and kept in a secluded home far away from the crowded town. She understood the dilemmas that both of them were facing. Their love would be considered sacrilege and they would both be put to death. So, she was willing to live the life of a secluded yet beloved wife of the Lord of Mordo though their marriage was solemnized only by their hearts and not by any priest.

They lived happily like this for about two years and soon, Ayesha, for that was Gabriella's mother's name, was pregnant. But, his father was pressuring him to marry someone eligible and he had to give into the pressures of those times and he married the woman who was his present wife from the Gascoigne family. Ayesha did not complain and knew that he had no option but to go along with the wedding.

"The time for your mother's delivery was drawing close. I had kept some trusted servants with her to help her during her pregnancy. But, it did seem that all was not well with her pregnancy. When the time came, she had a lot of pain and I could hear her screams as I waited in the outside room. The maid came outside after a few hours to tell me that you were born. You know today I realize that the sweetest sound that I have ever heard was the sound of your first cry! My heart swelled with happiness and unbridled joy!"

"But all was not well. Ayesha did not survive the childbirth. Before she died, she begged me to make sure that I give you a good life. In fact, she told me to bring you up as a Christian so you may have no confusions in your mind. She wanted you to marry a Christian and grow up with no enmity."

"But it was hard. Your Moorish roots were very strong. Your mother was a great warrior too and was skilled in sword-fighting and horse-riding and fencing. You carried it in your genes. I chose to let you have what you want because you were a part of my most beloved wife!"

"It was difficult to convince my Christian wife, Lady Irene of Galuven, but I had to. I threatened. I cajoled. I begged. I did everything in my power to convince her to take you as her child. Initially, she was reluctant. But, then she gave in. She had only one condition. No one was to know that the child was Ayesha's. She wanted everyone to believe that the child was hers! This surprised me because that is exactly what I wanted her to do. So, why was she asking as a return favor? That is when she told me about a love affair she had had during her younger wild days and she had gotten pregnant. In her fear, she had got the child aborted. But the procedure was done so badly that she had lost her ability to bear children. And she did not want this story to come out. So, she took on the role of her natural mother while I held her secret with me!"

Gabriella was crying as she heard the story of her parents. Both suffered so much of humiliation to keep her alive and happy. "Why the sudden change in attitude from the Queen?" asked Gabriella. She couldn't bear to call her mother any more.

"I don't know. Perhaps the resentment that she was holding down surfaced when she realized that her family will get a bit of the Moor blood when you married Ralph." This made sense. The mention of Ralph made her realize that she hadn't told her part of the story to her father.

Gabriella narrated her story and the Lord of Mordo felt sick that he was planning to get his beloved daughter married to a murderer. Yet, she did not understand why Ralph wanted her killed.

At that moment, the door opened and in walked Ralph, the Lady of Mordo, and Ralph's uncle who was supposed to have helped her get to Captain Philip.

The Queen's face was contorted in anger and Ralph was whimpering in fear. The uncle was also incredibly angry. "How did you escape from the killer? He never allowed his victims to escape," she screamed in helpless rage.

Haroun, who was in the shadows till now, emerged and on seeing him, the three faces went ashen. "What are you doing here?" blurted out Ralph.

"I came to get Gabriella justice."

The Lord of Mordo realized that it was his wife who had plotted to kill his daughter and in his rage, he lunged forth and drove his dagger through his wife's heart killing her instantly. Nobody got any time to stop this act. Ralph's uncle screamed in agony at seeing the Queen fall dead. His rage drove him towards the Lord of Mordo. But by this time, Haroun was alert and he stopped the uncle with his sword. He pinned him down and tied him to the chair. Ralph was looking on in horror as this scene unfolded. He looked like he would be happy to run away.

But Haroun had closed the door by now. The Lord of Mordo went towards Ralph's uncle and asked him, "Why did you want to kill my daughter?"

His face turned ugly with rage as he looked at Gabriella and said, "That is Moorish filth that is corrupting the Christian world! She had no right to live, leave alone live in luxury. She was becoming very popular with her people as well. She needed to be stopped and so I chose to get her killed. Your wife was completely on my side as she was becoming quite tired of your untiring love towards your concubine's daughter!"

The Lord of Mordo fell in a heap and turned to Gabriella and said, "My dear, run away from this place that has no place for love. Go with your Moor man and find your heaven of love. No one will ever understand love in Mordo where people prefer killing each other rather than loving each other."

'Take her away, Haroun. Her Moor roots have found her. Fate has a way with us! I tried hard to bring her up as a Christian but not a Christian filled with hatred but a Christian filled with love. Yet, the church she went to taught her to fight the Crusades. But when she met you, she learned to love. She is yours. Take her away while the people of Mordo and those of Gascoigne murder and plunder. Let them fritter this life that God has given them to love by killing and murdering. You take Gabriella away from here. She was not born to kill. She was born to love like her mother!"

# *Conclusion*

Ralph came forward and touched Gabriella by her shoulder. She screamed at him, "Don't you dare touch me. Why did you do what you did, Ralph? I thought we were good friends and shared all our thoughts. Why did you do what you did?"

Ralph looked into her forlorn eyes and hated himself. He had betrayed her trust and faith. She had come to him with her deepest desires and he did not realize that.

"Remember the night we ran away together? You asked me why I was so upset despite making preparations for my safe return. I couldn't respond to you nor look at you in your face. That is because if you had seen my face that night, you would have known that something was wrong and you would have gotten it out of me. I left after I met Haroun and showing him your tent knowing fully well that I will not be able to see your dead body."

"But I admit that for some time, I just got carried away by hatred. This man who is my uncle used me and I let him manipulate me into doing the things I did. When I first heard that you were the daughter of a Moor mother, I felt cheated. I loved you and wanted to marry you. But how could I marry a half-Moor? My Christian faith will never allow me to be happy by going against its tenets."

"Moreover, I thought I was doing it for the good of Christianity just like how you thought fighting a Crusade was for the good of Christianity. I thought I was killing an enemy. I was led to believe by him and your mother that you did not deserve to lead a Christian life because your mother was a Moor!"

"So, I became your enemy, Ralph? We have spent years of our childhood together. We share such beautiful memories of joy and happiness. And yet, a little bit of talk about religion was enough for you to decide to kill me? You could have come to me with my story, couldn't you? "

Then she stopped herself. If she had known that she was part-Moor before she met Haroun, wouldn't she have been ashamed of herself? Wouldn't she have been angry with her father for doing what he did? Sleeping with a Moor woman? Wasn't the meeting with Haroun the life-changing event of her life? Till then, did she know of love in its pure form?

Moreover, how could she be angry with Ralph for choosing to get her killed? She turned inward and asked herself, "Isn't that what I was planning on doing? Joining Captain Philip so I could kill and murder without compunction the likes of Haroun? I went to kill Moors and ended up falling in love with a Moor without even realizing that he was a Moor! And even when I realized the truth about him, my love did not diminish; it only became more passionate because of his ability to be honest and straightforward with me. He did not lie to me to win my love. He only told me the stark truth and let me decide what I wanted to do!"

Wasn't love more powerful than hate? Didn't Jesus Christ also preach love? Did he not say, "Love thy neighbor as much as you love yourself?" Why then do men hate one another so much? Does a man with a burnished skin feel love differently from a man with a white skin?

Gabriella was crying uncontrollably thinking all these thoughts. But deep in her heart, she knew that her father was right. As long as she and Haroun stayed in Mordo, they will be hunted. In the name of religion, these people will not let love to flourish and grow. They will spread hatred. Haroun and she needed to go away. She needed to give her true mother's death a purpose. She needed to love Haroun unconditionally and spread the word of love to all around.

She had no control over wars and battles. But she could control how she lived. She looked across to Haroun. His eyes were filled with her image and he was simply waiting for her to reach out!

She held her hand and he took it and both left the horrible scene through the same tunnel. The last glimpse that people of Mordo had of Gabriella and Haroun was they were riding into the horizon where the sun was rising and bringing hope and light to one and all!

# THE MOOR

## Book II of The Crusader Trilogy

before attempting any techniques outlined in this book.

By reading this document, the reader agrees that under no circumstances are is the author responsible for any losses, direct or indirect, which are incurred as a result of the use of information contained within this document, including, but not limited to, — errors, omissions, or inaccuracies.

# *Introduction*

It was 20 years since Haroun and Gabriella left Mordo. They married and settled in a Moor settlement named Aqlab. Even though Aqlab was predominantly Moor, the people of this region had chosen to stay away from the politics and enmities of the times, especially those that were driven by the Crusade Wars. They welcomed Moors and Christians equally with open arms. Aqlab was one of the rare places in Andalusia where both warring sects lived in peace and harmony.

It was for this express reason that Haroun chose to build a beautiful home for his beloved Gabriella in Aqlab. The money he had earned as an assassin came of use to him. He lavished love and attention on his beloved and gave in to every whim of hers. Gabriella returned her husband's love in equal measure and enjoyed pampering him with her excellent cooking skills.

She cooked, she cleaned, she knitted, she sewed and she did everything that at one time she would have thought it was not for her. Life was, indeed, inscrutable. Until she met Haroun, Gabriella wanted nothing else but to fight on the side of Christians in the Crusades. And when she met him, her life turned upside down. If Haroun had not come into her life by a queer twist of fate, she may not have known her true Moorish origins. For Haroun and his love, Gabriella happily left her beautiful home of Mordo, where her Christian father ruled from his marvelous Mordo Castle.

Today, she was happy that the sacrifice was worth it. Haroun and Gabriella were happy. He had employed the best architects and built a castle that was a magnificent replica of her home in Mordo. As they watched their new home take shape slowly but surely, Gabriella and Haroun were thrilled. She was able to leave behind the pain of having to abandon her father so abruptly, even though he was the one who pushed her to find a life of love and peace with Haroun away from the war-ridden Mordo.

The love between them grew stronger than before. It was as if their lives seemed to have a connection beyond this lifetime. They intuitively seemed to know each other's likes and dislikes and did everything in their power to keep their beloved happy. As the castle took shape, so did a new life in Gabriella's womb. Haroun couldn't decide whether he should be happier at having his beloved Gabriella with him or whether he should be happier about their symbol of love who was to be born.

In fact, happiness seemed to swell so much in

Haroun's heart, he was scared that he would burst with joy. Soon, a baby boy was born to Haroun and Gabriella and they chose to name him Tariq. Before their beautiful home was completely ready, Haroun and Gabriella were blessed with a second child, a beautiful baby girl whom they lovingly named Ayesha after Gabriella's natural mother.

Now, after 20 years of a happy life, Haroun and Gabriella were certain that their earlier lives were part of history and there was nothing more to fear from the past coming to create problems for them in the present.

# *Chapter 1*
## AQLAB

A qlab was a unique settlement where the effects of the Crusades were not felt at all. Here, the Moors and the Christians lived harmoniously without rift or rancor.

In fact, a large number of families in Aqlab had backgrounds similar to that of Haroun and Gabriella. The couple's fell in love with each other and owing to parental opposition and fears of religious persecution, they had to elope. Aqlab was a haven for such people. This community had been in existence over the last 100 years now and it had grown into a self-fulfilling settlement. Spread over several hundred acres of land, the people of Aqlab never knew what it was like to hate other people based on religion.

Churches and mosques were built side by side and, as an individual, you were free to choose any religion you liked. Until reaching the age of 15, the schools in Aqlab were mandated to teach the tenets of both Islam and Christianity.

When the children completed their 15 years of age, each could choose the religion he or she wished to follow. If the new adult wanted to, he or she need not follow any religion at all. There were many households where each spouse followed different religions and yet there were no issues between the couples on the basis of religion.

Other than the religions which were practiced at a very personal level by every individual of the city, the civic and social fabric of the city was governed by a law book made and regularly updated by the ruling clan of Aqlab, the Haisa Dynasty, with the help of a council which comprised of prominent and well-read citizens of Aqlab.

Haroun exhibited excellent leadership and warrior skills. He also showed a lot of insight while discussing changes in law based on the amazing amount of knowledge he had gained during his extensive travels all over the world. He and Gabriella with her royal background where she learned the art of ruling and administration became prominent members of this council. Haroun had completely given up his earlier profession. He and his wonderful family became a respected unit in the autonomous city of Aqlab.

During his earlier days, Haroun had traveled as far east as Turkey and, even there, he had heard of the wonders of land that lay even further east. Haroun had heard of countries which were rich and wealthy and had civilizations that dated even beyond the Roman dynasties. He had heard of faiths that were different from the Islam or Christianity. The learning from these travels had made Haroun the non-religious man he had become.

Now, Haroun had the opportunity to teach what he had learned during his travels to the young people of Aqlab. The city had two famous universities that attracted students from all over the world. Haroun taught history in these universities. His classes were very interesting and his students loved him. He added wit and humor to his lectures and everyone enjoyed coming to his classes. Even his assignments were a lot of fun to do.

While he taught, he also learned new things. The libraries at both the universities were full of books and manuscripts. He read a lot and found that much of what he had learned during his travel days was recorded in these books as well.

Moreover, Haroun had seen roads and drainage systems beautifully and efficiently engineered in the highly advanced city of Turkey. He liaised with the builders of Aqlab and brought those wonders into the city as well. Coming from rural Mordo wherein people used pots and pans to carry water from rivers and springs to their homes, Gabriella was initially overwhelmed by water pipes and taps that just needed to be turned for water to flow. She marveled at the knowledge of her husband and his ability to remember these details and ideas from his travels and replicate them in Aqlab for the good of the entire community.

"There is so much in this world to be happy about and to make others happy. Yet, I wonder why people choose to kill and loot and plunder in the name of religion," he said to his wife, one day when they were sitting and reading on the balcony of their beautiful home which they had christened Mordo Castle. The orange-red glow of the setting sun reflected off Gabriella's blue eyes and Haroun found his heart filled with love for his beautiful wife as she looked at him while he spoke.

The children and their friends were on the other side of the castle and they could hear their joyous laughter pervading the castle walls. Ayesha had turned 15 yesterday and there had been a large banquet thrown for her friends. All the prominent members including the royal family had attended the banquet. In fact, there were rumors that Ayesha had caught the fancy of Hassan, the second son of the present head of the royal clan. Haroun and Gabriella smiled at each other as they watched the two young people looking at each other coquettishly as they struggled with their adolescent yearnings.

Today, the day after the banquet, some of the children stayed back in the castle for two more days to spend time with the Mordo children, as they were referred to in the entire Aqlab community.

Hearing the peals of laughter coming from the direction of the swimming pool where the children were presently frolicking, Gabriella thought back to her own extremely happy childhood. She and her cousins, especially Cousin Ralph of the Gascoigne, would roam and explore the Castle of Mordo. She and Ralph knew every nook and cranny of the gigantic sprawling castle.

She felt the unshed tears in her eyes as she thought of that fateful day about 20 years ago when she realized that her favorite Cousin Ralph was the one responsible for trying to get her killed. Reading her mind, Haroun interrupted her thoughts with, "Let us forget the bad things of our past and let us not allow the ghosts from there haunt our lives. I agree that it was a great idea of yours not to burden our children by telling them about our lives before they were born. I am glad I agreed to your suggestion."

Haroun got up from his chair and walked towards his wife who was sitting on an exquisitely carved divan fitted with a soft cushion creating some embroidery. He sat beside her, lifted her face towards him, and said, "My dearest, your tears are wasted. Ralph doesn't deserve them and your father would not like you to have shed your precious tears on someone so vile."

"Come, let us go and watch our children enjoying themselves with their friends."

So saying, he got up and helped his wife to her feet and both walked to the eastern part of the castle which housed the little water pool made especially for their children. As the children saw their parents, they jumped up in glee and Tariq yelled, "Ma, get into the pool. The water is so cool and soothing."

She smiled at her handsome son, signaled her refusal, and sat on one of their chairs as she watched the children having fun. She exchanged meaningful glances with her husband as they both watched the surreptitious looks that Hassan and Ayesha gave each other. Ayesha was dressed in a long flowing robe and was sitting near her mother watching the boys playing. She saw Hassan's rippling muscles as he raced into the pool with the other boys. Hassan's sister, Amina, was with her nibbling on a sweetmeat and trying to catch Tariq's attention. He seemed oblivious.

None of these nuances were missed by the Mordo couple as they observed the children playing and laughing. Both were open to these adolescent phases of life and the community in Aqlab was open enough to allow boys and girls to mingle with each other within set limits and under the supervision of elders.

Haroun was especially happy that his daughter and son lived in a far more open environment to grow and develop than the girls of his childhood. Those girls were strictly forbidden to talk to anyone other men except their fathers, brothers and husbands. In fact, once the girls were married off, they were the properties of their husbands alone and they had to live in closed environs especially built for women in the castles. Haroun was very happy that his cherished daughter was having a much better childhood than the women of his times.

Yet, there was a residual fear that simply did not seem to leave him. Especially now when he saw his family growing and developing wonderfully and seeing Aqlab transform into a modern urban area with all facilities, these deep-seated fears seemed to gnaw at Haroun more than ever. The fear was actually well-grounded, he thought to himself.

Aqlab was safe and sound with the people inhabiting it free from the emotions of hatred and enmity. Yet, it was not immune to things happening outside of it.

News about the bloodshed in the Crusade Wars reached here too. While most of the inhabitants ignored the news, or treated it with the disdain it deserved, there was a small section of people who were slowly beginning to get attracted to the concepts of war and religion. These radical people belonged to two different sects, one on the side of Moors and the other on the side of the Christians.

Haroun knew all this because he was part of the selective few who had access to spy reports that reached the ruling clan. They were using these reports to target these radical people directly and trying to counsel them on the importance of religious peace for the happiness and welfare of Aqlab.

These fears and a nagging inexplicable idea from those brief days in Mordo when he had met and interacted with Ralph seemed to worry him more than ever. Haroun forcefully put those negative thoughts outside of his mind and continued to focus on the present.

# *Chapter 2*
## TARIQ

T ariq had a fairytale childhood filled with all the luxuries that money could buy. His parents were wealthy and influential people in the city of Aqlab and he himself received all the advantages of being born to them. His parents were ready to do anything for him and his sister loved him with all her heart and soul.

As a baby, he was round and cuddly and, as he grew up, he became the epitome of youth. Being brought up in an environment that had no problems to speak of, it was a wonder that Tariq did not turn into a spoilt brat. He was a responsible boy always ready to help the needy. He was quite sensitive to the economically poor section of his beloved city.

He always volunteered to work for the underprivileged during his school breaks or any other free time that he found. Like all the children living in Aqlab, Tariq also learned the tenets of both Christianity and Islam and realized early on that the founders of both the religions had only the good of men in their hearts. They only preached love and taught their followers to love anyone they came in touch with.

The education system in Aqlab was not closed in any way. It included the events that were happening in the contemporary times and so, Tariq and all his friends were well aware of the Crusade Wars that were being fought in the name of religion between the followers of Islam and Christianity.

As he grew older, Tariq and his father discussed a lot of philosophy and science. Like his father, he too wondered why men behaved the way they did when there were so many opportunities to be good and do good for everyone around. Moreover, Tariq always thought warring and fighting were a complete waste of time and it would be wiser to use this time to gain wisdom by reading books and learning and helping people whenever and wherever possible.

He considered himself very fortunate to have his home in the safe environs of Aqlab where people lived in peace and harmony and love abounded everywhere.

In school, Tariq and his friends studied history, language, philosophy, Mathematics and had a few science classes. Professors from different parts of the world had chosen to come to the famous Aqlab University to teach and learn. Other than academics,

Tariq had lessons in warrior skills including sword fighting, fencing, archery and horse-riding.

"Why do I need to learn fighting and archery, Father," he asked Haroun one day. "Especially when we live in a harmonious place like Aqlab where I have not even seen a street fight let alone a bloody battle?"

Haroun said, "Son, Warrior skills are not necessarily to go to war. They are also meant to be used for protection. Today, this city might be safe from marauding soldiers. However, no one has seen tomorrow. It is better to be prepared for any mishaps rather than sit back and think that nothing can go wrong. Moreover, will you not be physically fit and have powerful muscles when you practice your warrior skills?"

This final argument convinced Tariq and he made sure he did not miss a single class both in academics and in sports. But the subject that was closest to Tariq's heart was caring for the sick and wounded. He loved to learn about the various herbs and natural medicines that could help people overcome physical pain and diseases.

Many times, he brought home nearly-dead and wounded birds and animals and nursed them back to health. He read up all the books about medical care that were available in the university at Aqlab. Any free time he got, he would go to the forest and bring back curing herbs and plants, make tonics and ointments which he freely gave to anyone who needed them.

There was a particular professor who had learned much about of medical care during his travels to the eastern parts of the world and he often gave lessons to Tariq. Tariq loved nurturing and caring for the sick. He was extremely compassionate and hated hurting anyone. He loved everyone he came in contact with. When he was 15, Tariq chose to follow no religion and simply be on the side of morality and goodness.

On one cool summer evening, Tariq and his friends were practicing their sword fighting in the forest on the outskirts of the city. While some practiced sword fighting, others were racing their beautiful steeds. Out of the blue came one horseman chased by a group of men on horseback too. The hunted man kept looking back to see if his chasers were closing in.

Sadly, it looked like this hunted man's horse was badly wounded and the chasers were fast catching up. His face was covered fully and only his eyes were giving pleading looks to the boys playing in the clearing. That look was enough to egg Tariq and the boys into action. Being excellently schooled in fighting, the boys chased after the chasing men and after a short yet fierce battle, they were pushed beyond the boundaries of Aqlab.

The victim was still on his injured horse which had stopped even making an attempt to run. He was watching the ongoing battle through the slits in the scarf that covered everything else except his eyes. When Tariq returned after chasing out the hunting party, he walked across to the single horseman and as he went close enough, the horseman slid off the horse's back and fell into Tariq's arms.

As the horseman fell into Tariq's arms, the scarf came off from the face and what Tariq beheld left him speechless with wonder. As the headscarf fell off, a thick mane of beautiful black hair came cascading down Tariq's face and he saw the most marvelous and resplendent face he had ever seen in his life. He stared down mesmerized at the lady lying faint in his arms, her arms outstretched and her head falling back.

His friends who followed him shook him from his reverie. He stared dumbly at these friends and then at the wondrous girl in his arms. His friends made him lay her down on the soft grass and one of them sprinkled some water on her face. Her face wrinkled up when the cold water droplets fell on her and she slowly opened her eyes and saw a dozen pair of eyes staring down. She screamed and sat up. The boys moved out and gave her space and time to recover.

After a few minutes, Tariq who had got his wits back asked, "Who are you and why were those men chasing you?"

She gave Tariq a strange look and said, "My name is Imelda and I am the princess of Gascoigne. I am part of Captain Philip's army of Crusaders. I fell asleep while we were marching forward and I got left behind. As I was trying to find my way back, these men found me and tried to take advantage of me. I fought hard though my steed got hurt. When I couldn't manage to hold them back, I tried to get away and they continued to chase me. Thank you for your help in saving me from them."

He brushed off the gratitude and invited her to his home to take some rest before moving on. Secretly, he wanted to spend more time with her and get to know her. Tariq was, of course, sad that she chose to fight a war that he himself did not believe in. But, he thought to himself, "It has to be fate that she rode through this particular place when I was there so that I could find her. There must be a reason why my heart is still fluttering at the sight of her."

Not knowing what else to do and where else to go, Imelda accepted his invitation and they all rode back to Tariq's home. The other boys went to their own homes. As he helped Imelda off her horse, he called out, "Mother, I have brought someone who needs help."

Gabriella was used to such things. Her son would bring hungry children who needed to be fed, hungry and wounded animals for treatment and food. He was always bringing someone home for help. So, she called out from the kitchen, "Bring the person to the kitchen. Hot soup with fresh bread is ready to be served."

She got another place ready at the dining table in one corner of the large kitchen where the family usually had dinner together. Haroun and Ayesha were already sitting at the table waiting for the dinner. They all heard footsteps approaching and Tariq crossed the threshold and helped Imelda through the doorway.

All three of them looked up at the new entrant with smiling welcoming faces. Haroun and Ayesha got up to help the fatigued lady to the table while Gabriella stared at her, some deep-seated familiar inklings rising up in her mind. Imelda too smilingly thanked the three people who were helping her and then turned to the lady of the house. She looked at Gabriella and stopped short. She stared at her and said, "Aunt Gabriella!"

The four-people looked at her dumbstruck. None of them had ever met her and she was addressing Gabriella as Aunt! However, the familiar inklings in the mind of Gabriella crystallized as she recognized similar physical features on Imelda; the same winsome smile, the dark intense eyes, and the lithe body. The girl in front of her seemed like a copy of her Cousin Ralph. This thought hit Haroun too now and his gaze moved from his wife to the new lady not knowing what to do and what to say.

# *Chapter 3*
# THE ILLUMINATION

Haroun and Gabriella exchanged glances while their children stood in stunned silence. They had no clue that there were any family members living anywhere. They were told by their parents that both Haroun and Gabriella were orphans and had no other family to talk about. And here was this ravishing looking girl calling his mother Aunt Gabriella! What was happening? Were they fed with lies all their lives? How could this princess from Gascoigne be his mother's niece? So, did he have uncles and aunts and grandparents too?

Tariq gave both his parents questioning looks. Haroun took the lead after receiving a resigned look from his wife. He said, "Listen, children, let us finish dinner and I promise we will tell you everything in the morning."

Being the considerate host and caring person he was brought to be, Tariq reluctantly agreed and all sat at the table to eat a silent dinner. When the meal was over, Ayesha took Imelda to one of the guest rooms and settled her there. Then she came down to the drawing-room where she found her parents sitting on the couch with Tariq between them.

She went close to them and sat down on the floor and held their hands and said, "Mother, Father, I trust both of you implicitly. If there is something you have not told us, then there must be a valid reason. So, I plead that you shed your worried looks and tell us the truth so that we need not be afraid of anything unpleasant coming from the past."

Gabriella was so moved to hear her daughter talk in such a mature manner that she hugged her with happiness. However, she realized that Tariq was not in a very forgiving mood. He was really angry and resentful. The only reason he was sitting quietly was because he loved his parents too much. Haroun narrated the entire story of their past helped by Gabriella who filled in the gaps!

They had decided not to leave anything out. Starting from the night Gabriella chose to run away from her home in Mordo until the day they walked out of the Mordo castle driven by love and hope, Ayesha and Tariq were told about every detail of their parent's past. For a long time after the narration was over, the children sat unmoving in their places and had inscrutable expressions on their faces.

Haroun and Gabriella realized that there was a lot to

take in and their children would need time to come to terms with everything they had heard. After nearly an hour of silence where each of the four was caught up with his or her own thoughts, Tariq got up from his place and without saying a word, he walked out of the room and they heard his steps climb up the stairs and the sound of his bedroom door opening and then closing.

Ayesha too got up. But, she came towards her parents and hugged them, "There has been so much pain that both of you have taken up. Why did you not tell us and share the pain? I am your daughter, Mother. Did you not think I was capable of managing myself? Did you think that you have brought us up as such weaklings that we would not know how to share your burden?" Gabriella hugged her daughter back and both cried away the newly found pain.

"And thank you for naming me after an epitome of love. I feel so proud of my grandmother and I will do everything in my power to keep that love going." Gabriella's heart filled with love and pride for her daughter's maturity.

However, over Ayesha's shoulder, she saw her husband's eyes staring in the direction that Tariq took without saying anything. She knew that Tariq was not able to take in so much of emotion together and it worried her as much as it did her husband. They could do nothing at the present time about it. Right now, they needed to focus on their daughter who was opening up. They were happy that Ayesha could understand and relate to the dilemma as to why they chose to hide the sordid details from their children. They were happy that Ayesha could see that they did not want to burden their children more than they needed to. Ayesha then bade them goodnight and hugged them again and went up to her room.

But what about Tariq? Should they follow him to his room and see if he needed help? Should they give him more time to absorb what he had just heard? Or should they try to explain why they did what they did again? For the first time since they walked away from Mordo over twenty years ago, Haroun and Gabriella felt a piercing chill in their hearts!

"Maybe we should give him time, Gabe." She nodded her assent and both went to their room to rest for the night and waited for dawn to break. Suddenly from the direction of Tariq's room, they heard loud sounds. Both rushed and tried to open the door. It was locked from inside. But, they could hear things being thrashed around. They peeped in through one of the open windows and saw to their horror that all the things in the room were strewn all over.

Tariq was sitting with clothes disheveled on the bed. His eyes were red hot and he was staring at his parents with such hate that Haroun looked scared at the sight of his son! Tariq screamed through the window, "Go away from here! I don't want to talk to you. Please go away from here."

Gabriella said, "Don't do this to us, Tariq. We can talk and help you understand our situation better. Open the door and let us in." "No, mother," said Tariq. "Go away from here."

Haroun couldn't even start talking because Tariq's voice continued from inside, "And, tell that man to not even try to talk to me. I want to left alone." Haroun was stunned and he staggered back to his room closely followed by his dear wife who was trying her best to console him. He walked straight in and lay on his bed and turned away and let all the unshed tears of his life wet his pillow throughout the night. Gabriella was right with him throughout the night. The girls' rooms were on the other wing and thankfully they were not disturbed from their sleep.

The next day was as damp as their moods. It rained non-stop. Imelda came down for breakfast looking refreshed and radiant. The others hadn't come down yet. Gabriella couldn't help feeling a sense of happiness to see her beautiful niece. They hugged and sat down. Gabriella poured some fresh milk into a huge glass and handed it over to Imelda. She sipped the frothing liquid and looked at her aunt.

"So, how did you recognize me?"

"I have seen many of your portraits in the Mordo Castle. You haven't changed much."

"Grandfather misses you a lot and he keeps talking about you whenever I visit Mordo. To be honest, my desire to join Captain's Philips army to be part of the Crusades stemmed from listening to those stories." Imelda blushed and continued, "Maybe I was hoping to meet the love of my life the way you did." Gabriella laughed and asked, "So, did you?" Imelda laughed along with her aunt and did not respond to the question.

But, tell me, Aunt Gabe, why did you leave Mordo? Grandfather talks to me about everything else except that!" Ignoring that question, Gabriella asked, "Did you fight in any of the battles?"

"Yes, I fought in just one battle and the blood and

gore of the scene left me unnerved! I realized this was not what I wanted to do for the rest of my life. The sight of two dead bodies was enough to tell me that wars are such a waste of time. I was riding with these thoughts in my mind when I got left behind and the marauders came after me. And your son saved me from them!" She smiled as she watched Tariq enter the kitchen.

Gabe's heart skipped a beat when she saw her son. He nodded to Imelda and did not even acknowledge his mother. Gabriella thought her heart is going to burst with sadness. Not a single day had gone by when Tariq did not come squealing into the kitchen every morning and hugged her before he took his place at the breakfast table. And today, he was so cold! In the last 17 years since he was born, she had never seen this face of her son! Gabriella was devastated!

Haroun walked in at that moment and immediately caught his wife's expression and realized that Tariq was not alright. When he saw his father enter, Tariq served himself some breakfast and took the plate and walked out of the kitchen. Haroun's face reflected the deep grief he felt too.

Imelda felt awkward in this situation though she did not understand what was going on. Instead of making it more difficult for her aunt and uncle, she asked for permission to take her breakfast and join Tariq. They heartily agreed thinking that the presence of a stranger might help their son.

After breakfast, everyone went about their work and when they met again for breakfast the next day, yesterday's scene was repeated. Tariq took his breakfast plate and walked out though this time, Imelda made no attempt to follow him.

"Did Tariq talk to you yesterday?" asked Gabe.

"Oh yes! He asked me all about the Crusade wars and where Captain Philip was stationed and he wanted to know every gory detail about the battle and the battle scenes. In fact, I felt relieved after I unburdened my experiences to Tariq," said Imelda.

The faces of Haroun and Gabriella paled at this news! Had their story changed the way Tariq thought? Did he want to take revenge by joining the crusading forces? She had to stop this! Gabriella walked out and as Haroun rose to follow her, she said, "I think it would be better if I went alone and spoke to him." Haroun nodded his agreement and sat back in his seat.

A concerned Imelda asked, "Is everything alright, Uncle Haroun?" Hearing the word uncle for the first time in his life filled Haroun's heart with happiness.

He smiled at Imelda, "Yes, dear! Just difficult phases of growing up! Ayesha, why don't you take Imelda and show her around the castle?"

The two girls got up and walked out the door and Haroun could hear his daughter's excited voice, "Let me first show you the pool that my father created for us." When the girls left, Gabriella called two of the domestic helpers and asked them to go and clean up Tariq's room and requested them not to talk about the state of the room to their daughter. The couple had become well-loved and well-respected in the community and the helpers realized their need for discretion and happily agreed.

# *Chapter 4*
## MOTHER, SON AND FATHER

Gabriella followed her son outside. He sat on one of the benches in the spacious lawn nibbling at his breakfast with a thoughtful expression on his face. He did not hear his mother come up from behind him. He only realized she was there when she placed her hand gently on his shoulder. He became rigid and his body exuded a coldness that Gabriella found frightening.

She came around and sat next to Tariq. He tried getting up to walk away. She held his hand and gently pulled him to sit down again.

"Tariq, we are very sorry for having not shared our past with you earlier. But, we thought it best not to hurt you with the stories of pains and agonies that we went through. We wanted to put the past behind us and didn't want it to haunt our beautiful present."

Tariq looked at his mother and his eyes flashed so much anger that she was stunned. She realized that keeping the past from Tariq was not a good thing to do. She wondered what aspect of the past angered him so much. This time, when Tariq got up to move away from his mother, she couldn't find the courage to hold him back. She had seen the hatred for her in his eyes and she simply did not know how to handle hatred from his beloved son.

As Tariq moved away, she saw Haroun emerge from the big bush in the corner of the lawn and come towards her. He came over and sat down beside and she realized his eyes were damp too. They hugged each other hoping to find solace. Both of them were desolate. While they were happy that Ayesha understood their dilemma, they were devastated that Tariq was not willing to forgive them.

Haroun made another attempt at talking to his son. He followed his son who had by then reached the balcony of the topmost floor in the Castle. He was looking over the intricately carved parapet and was lost in thought. He seemed to lean over so much that Haroun thought he was trying to fall off. In a fit of panic, the father ran and held his son and pulled him off from the edge of the parapet.

Completely surprised and annoyed by this move, Tariq sprung away from his father's touch and brushed him off in a rough manner. Haroun saw the same hatred in his son's eyes that he had seen when Gabriella was talking to him before. He stood erect and despite being deeply stung by his son's behavior, he approached him and said, "We are really sorry for hurting you so much, Tariq. Our intentions were to keep you safe, not to hurt you like this. What do you want us to do to make you feel better and forgive us?"

"I cannot treat you as my parents anymore!"

These cruel words stung Haroun so much that he thought his heart would break under the agonizing pain of such obvious repulsion from his only son!

"You are an assassin! You have killed and murdered people for money. How can you live with that thought? Don't those pictures of blood and gore that were your making return to haunt you at night? How many people have you killed? Is this house and our clothes and our food made with the blood money? I am ashamed that I have lived for so long eating and drinking from the wealth created by your killing and massacre! What you did cannot be forgiven! Go away! I never want to set eyes on you again!" So saying, Tariq ran down the stairs and Haroun watched in horror as he saw his son riding away on his horse, every step of the horse taking Tariq farther away from him literally and figuratively.

Haroun heard footsteps and saw his wife standing there with tears streaming down! She ran forward and hugged her husband and tried her best to console him. Whatever else they expected, they did not expect Tariq to hate his father for his assassin days! They did not realize that Tariq had been brought up in such an ideal environment that he believed that killing and murdering were simply unforgivable and he couldn't bring himself to see his own father killing people for money!

The couple was grief-stricken. They were just happy that Ayesha did not hear this conversation. However, even this joy was short-lived as they saw their daughter walking towards them with Imelda following close behind. Now, their grief was out in the open and they did nothing more to hide the pain of being hated by their own son.

All the achievements since they came to Aqlab seemed to disappear into oblivion and Haroun could only see himself as the assassin who killed mercilessly for money. "How come I didn't hate myself as much as until today? Did my son need to tell me what a cruel past I had? What right did I have to bring an innocent child into this world and tell him that your father was a killer for money?" All the philosophy lessons he took and those he taught seemed so meaningless now that his son despised him with such vehemence!

He even felt estranged from his wife because Tariq did not seem to find as much fault with her as he did with his father. He hated his father and he didn't despise his mother so much. There was not a word against Gabriella that Tariq spoke. He only taunted his father for his blood money! Haroun felt alone in this world. He felt as alone as he did when his mother passed away! He felt like an abandoned child who no one wanted!

He walked away slowly from his wife and daughter and went down the stairs, a man totally lost and helpless and alone and loveless.

Gabriella was shattered to see her family break up in front of her eyes. But, she was not going to let this happen. She knew that father and son simply needed time to get over their pain. Mother and daughter exchanged pained looks and Imelda simply stood by not knowing what to do.

She said, "If I hadn't come to this side of Andalusia, all this would not have happened! It is my fault that a beautiful family is going through so much of heartbreak. I should not have left home at all. I have not been able to be a good warrior. And the love that I found has lost himself in his own gloom and I am the reason for his gloom!"

Ayesha and Gabriella looked at Imelda with surprise. Imelda blushed and said, "Yes, Aunt Gabe. I have found my love the way you did. I realized how you must have felt when you first laid eyes on Uncle

Haroun when I first laid eyes on Tariq. I cannot think of a life without him and now I am feeling that I am the cause of the pain in this wonderful home."

Suddenly, Gabriella felt that it is only a matter of time for Tariq to see the truth of his father's love and forgive him for something that happened when no one control over their lives. Gabriella beckoned Imelda close and said, "That is the best thing I have heard since last night! I am so glad that Tariq has someone like you to love him. Go after him and show him the way of the world. He has seen too much of an idealist life that he doesn't want to accept that wars and agonies of wars exist outside of his comfortable Aqlab. Go and tell him and speak about the horrors of the outside world. He will slowly accept the outgrown weaknesses of his father as well. Go, child, go do me this favor. Find Tariq and speak to him and bring him back home!"

# *Chapter 5*
## TARIQ AND IMELDA

Imelda was thrilled to hear her aunt's suggestion. She had fallen head over heels in love with Tariq. The feeling had started off as a simple revelation when she first saw him look down at her as he caught her falling from her injured horse. Then, after knowing that she had unwittingly stumbled into the house of Aunt Gabriella whose stories she had grown up with and realized that Tariq was her cousin once removed, she knew that he was her destiny.

There might be a temporary misunderstanding in the family right now because of old hidden stories being revealed. Yet, she knew that this family's bonds were very strong and built on an unbreakable foundation of love and affection; the kind of deep love that will come out stronger after undergoing an especially testing period.

And, Imelda realized that she now wanted to be part of this lovely family. Her parents knew no love between them and theirs was a marriage of convenience to build and strengthen Gascoigne's political power. Her father, Ralph was a quiet contented man; but her mother, the strong-willed Lady Griselda from the Mordo family, was very ambitious. She drove her husband to support the Crusades and give temporary asylum to traveling Crusaders when they pass through Gascoigne.

This was hardly based on love for the soldiers and was more because of attracting the attention of the prominent rulers of that area who were very close to the Pope. She was using her husband's strategically located kingdom to get favor from the Pope so that Gascoigne will grow and expand. Lady Griselda wanted Gascoigne to become more powerful that Mordo so as to be able to annex it.

Growing up in this kind of a loveless environment, Imelda was overjoyed to see that the ideal family she often dreamed did exist here in Aqlab and she was getting an opportunity to be part of this beautiful family. She did see the attraction that Tariq had for her. Although there was some amount of disruption in the family love for the moment, Imelda knew this sadness to be a temporary situation only. It is not possible for people who love each other dearly to be separated for very long.

She followed Tariq and found him sitting near a stream in the forest nearby deep in thought. His horse was tethered close by. She came and sat down next to him and touched him gently on his shoulders. He turned to see the girl of his dreams sitting next to him and his heart was filled with happiness and love.

After the past of his parents was revealed to him, the only thing that hurt him was the fact that his father was a paid assassin at one point in time. Tariq was sickened by the images that kept running in his head about how his father would have killed and maimed people just so that he could earn money. Since the time Tariq heard about his father's past, he was thinking, "How could he live so peacefully and so contentedly despite knowing that his hands were responsible for the deaths of so many people? How could he talk of peace and love and the importance of peace when he himself had killed so many people and that too only for the sake of making money? And how could his mother love him despite knowing that he was an assassin and in fact, had been hired to kill her too?"

Tariq couldn't find answers for these tormenting questions in his mind. Until now, he had placed his father on a pedestal and thought he was the most perfectly noble man that existed and when he was told that his father was nothing more than a paid assassin until a few years ago, the pedestal he had built came crashing down and he found he couldn't look his father in his eyes. He was ashamed of being Haroun's son and he found this emotion so deep-seated that for the last few days, he had simply avoided talking to his parents hoping and praying that this feeling of hatred towards his parents, especially his father, will ebb away with time.

Then, this morning when his father tried to approach him, Tariq realized he couldn't hold on to his emotions and he burst forth and asked his father all those questions that were bothering him. He could the pain in his father's eyes and this angered him even more because he hated to see his father in such a pitiable situation. He stormed out of the house, got on his horse, and rode off towards the forest which gave him a lot of peace and solace.

He was sitting near the stream and thinking all these thoughts when Imelda came by and sat down next to him. He was so overcome with emotion that he turned and hugged Imelda hoping to use the love he was feeling for her to bury the hatred he was feeling for his father. Imelda hugged him back and then pulled him away to see tears streaming down his cheeks. She gently wiped them away and held him again till he calmed down.

After a few minutes, she said, "Tariq, please do not consider me to be very forward. But I have to tell you that I have fallen for you from the first moment I saw you!"

Tariq was so happy at this that he laughed heartily and said, "Imelda, the same goes for me too. When I saw the dark luscious hair cascading down against my face as you slid off the horse, I knew I was in love. The look in your dark intense eyes only confirmed my love for you!"

They smiled, laughed, and were so happy that there were able to be so candid with each other.

Soon, however, Imelda asked about why he was being so cruel this father and his eyes darkened with hate. She shrunk at this and said, "I am sorry, Tariq. I did overhear your conversation with your father this morning. Ayesha was showing me around the castle and we were just stepping onto the terrace when we heard you. I wanted to walk away because I thought it was a very private family issue and I did not have a right to intrude. But, Ayesha held me back."

"You know, she is as devastated as you are, Tariq. Have you asked yourself how she doesn't see what you see? Is it because she loves her father more than you do? If that is the case, isn't the fault in your shortage of love?"

Tariq was livid that the girl he wanted to spend the rest of his life with was finding fault with him. And yet, he paused to think about what she said. "Was the love for my father so flimsy that anything could break it? But, realizing the fact of his father being an assassin was a powerful emotion too and was capable of turning love to hatred"

He looked at Imelda and said, "Let's forget about my father. You tell me more about your experiences in the battles that you witnessed."

# *Chapter 6*
## CAPTAIN PHILIP AND HIS CRUSADING ARMY

Imelda asked Tariq if he knew about the Order of Malta and its knights. When Tariq said he was hearing about this order for the first time. Imelda went on to give him a brief description of this order.

The Order of Malta was founded for the primary purpose to care for sick pilgrims in Jerusalem. The Order of Malta was granted approval by the Caliph of Egypt to build a hospital, a church, and a convent in Jerusalem more than a century and a half ago. The hospital became an autonomous body under the approval of the Pope and it ran its offices under its own constitution without interference with any other religious or political body.

The knights of the Order of Malta were all religious and were bound by the oath of obedience, poverty and chastity. Captain Philip was a knight of this order and was given a part of the territory within Andalusia to manage the Crusades there and also handle the medical care of the wounded soldiers.

Imelda said, "I heard a lot of stories about your mother from your grandfather, Lord Esmour Martyn of Mordo. I was deeply moved by her courage to do things differently and not to accept everything simply because someone was telling her to. I wanted to be like Aunt Gabriella. I worshiped her and begged Grandfather to tell me everything about her. I already knew about your father being what he was before he met your mother. I was so moved by their story of love that I wanted that to repeat in my life and in the hope of finding true love, I learned the art of warfare."

"As your mother had already set a precedent of making warriors of women too in Mordo and Gascoigne, I didn't have to run away in the middle of the night to do want your mother wanted to do. I was given permission and a lot of help to reach Captain Philip's army that was stationed in the same place as it was 20 years ago. I reached the place Aunt Gabriella couldn't reach."

"But horrors of war that I witnessed were too much for me to bear. It was much too agonizing for me to remember the true cause of the Crusades. I thought it better to give up the cause rather than spread so much of pain, heartache and sadness through war."

The religious fervor has been totally mutilated and everyone is wreaking havoc cruelly, mercilessly and without reason. The number of wounded soldiers was increasing every day and there was no one to look after them. The soldiers who were not wounded were so proud of their achievements that they treated people with arrogance.

Every time a battalion of soldiers passed through a settlement, the women and children were the worst affected. They were raped, villages were plundered, and children were not spared either. The pedophiles in the marauding army used religion to create atrocities on women and children and none had the courage to fight them.

Fires that were created as weapons spread all over and consumed entire villages. The wounded soldiers did not get sufficient treatment and their infected wounds killed them sooner rather than later. If they had had access to medical care, perhaps, the number of wounded soldiers would have been less in number, Imelda said.

Many of the dead soldiers did not receive a funeral. Their bodies lay rotting on the battlefield and these rotting bodies spread more diseases than ever. More people were dying of diseases like small pox, measles, dysentery and plague than ever. It is a horrifying sight as you travel through Andalusia. These inhuman conditions made it very difficult for Imelda to continue feeling any idealism for war. She wanted to end and stop it rather than feel proud of participating in the Crusades.

"Your mother was very fortunate to have met your father before she reached Captain Philip's camp. She never needed to see the horrors of war that I got to see. She only saw love and happiness. Yes, some cruel facts of her life did come forward because of this. But, she refused to be taken in by the sadness and instead used the love from your father to make her life into what it is" said Imelda, her eyes full of sadness as she thought back to those horrible days of the war.

Tariq put his arms around her shoulders and tried to console her and told her, "Forget those days, Imelda. Put them out of your head. They are in the past. Let us look forward to our life together."

Imelda was pleased with this and said, "Can you put away the earlier days of your father's life as well? Then, we can live together as one big, happy, loving family?

To this, Tariq replied, "No, Imelda. I cannot do that. What he did was far more horrifying than fighting in a war! He used his killing skills to earn money and he had no other noble motive. He is a killer and I cannot forget that. I cannot go back to face him again. I need to do something that will help me dissolve the horrible images that keep coming up when I think of my father."

"And by enlisting to Captain Philip's army, I know the exact thing that will act as a repentance for all the killings of my father," said Tariq. "I am going to join Captain Philip's army."

Horrified at this, Imelda looked at him and said, "How can joining Captain Philip's Crusading army absolve the sins of your father? Wouldn't it add to them? Did I not tell you just now about the horrible acts committed by ruthless soldiers irrespective of which side they chose to fight for? Aren't those images of raped women and children sufficient to make you want to run as far away as possible from those situations instead of going toward them?"

Tariq put his hand over Imelda's mouth and told her, "I am not going to fight in the war. I am going to join his hospital to care for the sick and wounded. I realized just now that if I can at least save a few men and women from death by tending to their wounds, I could be countering a few murders that my father did as an assassin. It makes sense, doesn't it?"

Imelda was stupefied by this revelation. Her love for Tariq increased even more. Although she did not blame Haroun for his choice of life before he met her Aunt Gabriella, Imelda thought this would be a great way for Tariq to go see the outside world, move away from the idealist world in Aqlab. This might help him forgive his father whose childhood was nowhere as beautiful as Tariq's.

She immediately said, "That is such a noble idea, Tariq. I want to join you too. I only looked at the horrors and pain and I did not even realize I should do something for the sick and wounded. And here, you only heard about the horrors and you wanted to immediately do something constructive. I applaud you for your nobility and feel so fortunate that a person like you wants to spend the rest of his life with me. Let me come with you. I will introduce you to Captain Philip and he will find something good for us to do. He does need people to work for the wounded and there are fewer people who volunteer for that kind of work than to fight. He will be happy to receive your help."

Tariq was happy to hear this and said, "That is the second best thing I have heard in the last two days. Come, let us go, pack a few things, and leave at once."

Imelda was puzzled! She asked, "The second best thing? What was the first best thing then?"

Tariq looked lovingly at her and said, "That you had fallen for me!"

113

Imelda smiled at him and blushed. They both got up and made their way towards home.

"We can tell Aunt and Uncle and leave. They will be happy too."

"No! We will leave without telling them. I want my father to feel what it is to lose a loved one. He should feel what the families of his victims felt!"

"But that is so cruel, Tariq."

"If you think so, then don't come with me. I will find my own way."

Imelda looked at the stern expression on Tariq's face and realized that nothing she said would convince him otherwise. And she wanted to go with him. She wanted to stay with Tariq for two reasons; one because she promised her aunt that she would bring him back home and two because she felt responsible for the split in the family and she wanted to be the one to set it right.

So, she agreed with him to go away without telling her aunt and uncle. When they reached the castle, it was already dark and everybody seemed to be asleep. Tariq quickly and quietly went up to his room, packed a few clothes, and left. Imelda went to Ayesha's room and picked up some of her clothes because she had none of her own.

They met again outside the castle and got onto the horse and rode away into the darkness. From the window of the master bedroom, Haroun and Gabriella watched their beloved son moving farther away from them. While Gabriella openly cried, Haroun held onto his grief so that he could console his beloved wife.

Under the pretext of picking up some clothes from Ayesha's room, Imelda had gone to her uncle and aunt and told them their entire plan. She realized that they would understand their son's dilemma and would let him do what he wanted to do so that he could forget the past more easily than now. Also, both of them realized that their son needed to see the cruelties of the outside world to become stronger.

# *Chapter 7*
## THE HOSPICE FOR THE WOUNDED AND THE SICK

After a day's journey, Tariq and Imelda reached Captain Philip's camp. They stayed in the Gascoigne camp where volunteer soldiers from Imelda's kingdom were put up. These friends were very happy to see Imelda again. After she disappeared sometime ago, everyone in the Gascoigne camp was worried and, in fact, had lost hope of her safe return.

They presumed the worst and thought either wild animals killed her or maybe she had fallen victim to some marauders. They had searched the area the night of her disappearance and when they found no sign of her or her horse, they sent word to Lord Ralph and he was now on his way to the camp hoping to find his beloved daughter.

Imelda was happy on hearing the news that her father was on his way to Captain Philip's camp. She thought it would be a great thing for him to meet the man whom she wanted to marry and settle down with. Yet, she was a little worried that some more

116

ghosts of the past might be revealed to Tariq and he might get more agitated than before. She put these thoughts aside for the moment and simply reveled in the evening dinner that she was partaking with her Gascoigne friends who are all enjoying their conversation with Tariq.

Tariq, Imelda realized, was made of a sunny disposition and he never let his personal problems come in the way of being nice to her friends. He regaled them with stories of Aqlab and his life there. She noticed that he carefully avoided bringing the topic of his father into his stories and kept his stories to life in the university there and the learning there especially the art of medical care which was a novelty for her people.

Nobody really knew that medical care could be a profession or something that really mattered. Until now, everybody believed that one continued to work and toil as long as one could. And if you contracted a disease or fell ill, you simply waited for death to come and take you. Hygiene and other aspects of medical care were unheard of and it fascinated the young men and women of Gascoigne that the sick could be treated with medicines to alleviate pain and diseases could be prevented from spreading by simple rules of hygiene and cleanliness.

After dinner, Imelda took Tariq to meet Captain

117

Philip in his tent. Word had reached him that Imelda was safe and he happily received her and welcomed Tariq heartily too. Captain Philip was a religious monk who managed the affairs of the Order of Malta's branch in Andalusia. He managed recruiting and training volunteers for the Crusades. One thing that was different about the Order of Malta from the other monasteries of the day was the importance of hospice care, however little, that was given to wounded soldiers.

The knights of the Order of Malta fought wars too but also made an effort to look after wounded soldiers and pilgrims. When Captain Philip heard of Tariq's request to be taken as a volunteer for hospice care, he was quite surprised. He was still to come across young men who preferred to care for the sick rather than fight a war. Being a warrior and dying a warrior's death was considered the ultimate sign of manhood. And here was a young man who preferred to live in the squalor and dirt to treat the sick, thought Captain Philip. He was extremely happy to have Tariq on board. They spoke at length about Aqlab.

Captain Philip said, "Yes, I have heard of this unique city and I believed no one would want to leave the peace and harmony that existed there to come and take part in a war. Why did you leave your home for this?" asked Captain Philip. Even though he was a knight, Captain Philip was a man of God too and he recognized a deep pain in Tariq's eyes. Something stirred in his heart and he asked Tariq about his parents.

"I would prefer not talking about it, Captain," said Tariq as he lowered his eyes not wanting to meet the gaze of Captain Philip. The captain also did not press further at that point in time and chose to move on instead about the arrangements of the hospital. They decided to ride out together early the next morning to inspect the hospital which was about five miles away from the camp.

After a few more minutes of talking to the Captain, Imelda and Tariq came back to the Gascoigne camp and being thoroughly enervated lay down and fell asleep even before their heads hit the mattress.

The next day dawned bright and clear. After washing up from a stream that flowed nearby and after having some hot soup and bread for breakfast, Imelda and Tariq went to Captain Philip's tent. The captain was waiting for them ready for the ride to the hospital area. The three of them were on separate horses and they rode in silence. When they reached the hospital area, the first thing that hit Tariq was the stench of death.

There was death on everyone's faces. He had never

seen such misery in his life and suddenly Tariq wanted to run away and go back to the comforts of his beautiful home in Aqlab. He recalled his father's childhood and suddenly he realized that his father must have felt what he was feeling right through his young days, hopeless and worthless. Tariq realized this was the first time in days when he was thinking of his father without a feeling of resentment.

He shook off these feelings and decided to focus on the task at hand. He looked all around. There was filth everywhere. The wounds on the soldiers were open and festering. The faces of the people were lifeless even though they were not dead. The people had defecated and there was no one to clean up after them. The smell of human excrement pervaded the atmosphere. While Tariq and Imelda closed their noses ostensibly, Captain Philip seemed to be made of sterner stuff. He looked at them and gave a knowing smile. He somehow thought that this beautiful couple may not survive here for very long and his meaningful glances to them seemed to convey these feelings.

Tariq realized what Captain Philip was thinking and he immediately took his hand away from his nose and bravely walked around the long corridor with dirty and near-dead people lying uncared for on either side. The inside of the hospital was even worse. The stench was even more horrible and the lack of air made the stink almost unbearable. A few reluctant workers were trying to clean the wounds of some of the patients and their work was hardly worth talking about. Even the presence of Captain Philip did little to make them work harder. It seemed that the most hopeless people who had no other skill came to the hospital as volunteers. These people, at least, got a meal in return for doing some voluntary work. If they stayed behind at home, they would die of starvation.

Tariq realized the hopelessness of the scenario. But, something within him stirred. It was a small ripple that seemed to start off from the depths of his heart and was waiting to turn into a huge wave exploding outside his body and clearing and washing the dirt and squalor all around and leaving the area spotlessly clean.

Imelda saw the sparkle in Tariq's eyes and was so happy to see life in them again that she forgot all about the stench and filth and simply wanted to do everything she could to keep that sparkle intact. The change in Tariq's demeanor did not go unnoticed by Captain Philip either and he thought, "Maybe I should be patient and give this couple more time."

He left them there, as while showing them around, he had told the volunteers that Tariq and Imelda would be running this hospice care and everyone had to take orders from them. There was a small ripple of excitement passing through the small group of volunteers as they looked in awe at the strapping young lad and the beautiful lady who had chosen to give up a life of luxury to help them run and manage this hospice that was on the brink of collapse.

# *Chapter 8*
## IMMERSED IN WORK

Tariq was young, only 17 years of age. But something about his demeanor and face made people look up to him. He was able to draw out the best in people. Even in the university at Aqlab, peers and juniors automatically turned to him whenever there was a need for a leader both in study and sports activities. He felt that same urge to take the lead and make the people around do their best.

Tariq smiled at each of the volunteers, not all of them young and strapping (if they were strapping they would have been soldiers). But each of them was capable of doing a lot, Tariq realized. They only lacked motivation and drive. They were a mere ten in number. The presence of this young and beautiful couple seemed to increase their energy levels to inexplicable limits. They all came forward and nodded to Tariq and Imelda and waited for orders.

Tariq said, "By the end of seven days, this hospice care is going to become spotlessly clean and we are going to do it together."

The power of this certainty reverberated through the

air and every sick and wounded person who heard it also believed in its truth. Tariq had found a calling and he was going to do his best to answer that calling. He now had a purpose in life. He wanted to undo at least a few deaths that his father so callously had undertaken in his rash youth. Once, he did what he wanted to, maybe he would find the strength to forgive his father too.

Tariq and Imelda, along with the volunteers, started work immediately. There was a sparkling spring flowing right behind the hospice care. Whatever his professor at the Aqlab taught him seemed to come back to him like magic. He remembered his professor telling him how in one of the earliest known medical books that he had read about disinfectants, quicklime used in the correct proportions was an excellent disinfectant. Tariq had read that book which was available at the library there and today he was able to recall those details without a doubt.

There was a lot of quicklime that Captain Philip gave from his armory. Then, quicklime was also used as a weapon to spray on enemy soldiers. Tariq first got six of the ten volunteers to bring pots, pans and other cleaning items including the quicklime from Captain Philip. He taught them how to use quicklime as disinfectants demonstrating how it had to be mixed in the water for cleaning.

The excitement was infectious. The volunteers were happy to be infected with such fervor and excitement. They always lived in fear of picking up dysentery or some other deadly disease from the patients lying all around. Now, they worked very hard to scrub and clean every part of the hospice care building taking it turn by turn.

First, they transferred the patients from one part of the building to the courtyard. They then cleaned that part and scrubbed with water laced with quicklime and the smell of the chemical pervaded the entire floor livening up many of the sick and wounded soldiers. They brought back the patients and took the next batch outside while they cleaned the emptied part of the hospice building. In one day, only two parts of the entire building could be cleaned. But, at the end of the day, when they saw how wonderfully and spotlessly clean the floor was, they were wanting to work the entire night to clean up the second floor.

Tariq taught the remaining four volunteers and Imelda how to clean the wounds of the sick, how to nurture and care for the ill, how to cheer them up, how to treat them with love and respect, and how to give them the will to get better.

"A large part of the treatment is dependent on the

patient. If he or she does not want to get better, no herb or medicine will help. Medicines and herbs are only active when the will of the sick is mixed with them. Else, they are useless. Show them love and care and they will find a purpose to live and then the medicines will work their wonders." This was Tariq's first lesson to his volunteers.

The sick and wounded soldiers were amazed at the way the volunteers smiled their way through the strenuous and difficult work. No one felt bad to even clean up human excrement when Tariq demonstrated how it could be done. They looked awestruck at this energetic man and did everything they could to get a smile or a word of appreciation from Tariq.

The people worked untiringly taking breaks only for small meals. An entire floor and all the patients living in it were clean and happy to be alive at the end of the first day. The volunteers were ready to work overnight and make the hospital clean even earlier than the seven days that Tariq was talking about in the morning.

Tariq stopped them from overworking and told them to rest. "Don't overdo it. Remember you need to work like this for another month or so before the hospital can become what I envision it to become. And make sure you clean yourselves. Wash your hands and legs and with the disinfectant water and then bathe in the spring before having your dinner. I need my hardworking volunteers healthy and ready for more hard work tomorrow," he smiled. They were so enthused with his bright wide smile that they looked ready to lay down their lives for him.

Imelda watched this and realized that Tariq was a born leader. And what could you expect? The son of ruling Christian and an erstwhile powerful Moor clan could be nothing but a leader, she thought to herself. In one day, the building and inhabitants looked different. The first scene of the morning was wiped out from her mind as she saw everybody retiring for the night and waiting for dawn to break so that they could continue to do the good work that was started today by their beloved leader, Tariq.

Tariq and Imelda washed up too and after eating a simple meal of hot and healthy bone broth made by one of the volunteers with the help of Imelda, they both got onto their horses, reached the Gascoigne camp and fell asleep even faster than they did yesterday. Today was a satisfying day and sleep came happily to Tariq and Imelda.

# *Chapter 9*
## TARIQ'S FAMILY ARRIVES

T he next day dawned and Tariq and Imelda were up and about even before sunrise. They got ready and before breakfast could be served in the Gascoigne camp, they rode off together to the hospice building. It was for a very good reason that the hospice building was kept far away from the soldier camps. Nobody wanted the soldiers to catch any deadly infectious disease.

No one wanted to be anywhere near the hospice area. The only one who visited there occasionally was Captain Philip who went to see if anything needed to be done that required his approval. Anyway, death did not need anyone's approval. He had visited the hospice after nearly three months yesterday with Tariq and Imelda. The war-related tasks and work took up so much of his energy and time that he hardly had anything to give dying people except his prayers for a peaceful and painless death.

And here was Tariq already gone to the hospice without even waiting for breakfast to be served. He was overcome with emotion. But, he had work to do and decided to focus on today's battles and battle tactics with his commanders and soldiers and he pushed Tariq, Imelda, and the hospice out of his mind.

So, here was Captain Philip fighting one kind of battle and there was Tariq fighting another kind of battle. Each day at the hospice created new problems and the volunteers realized that the first day was the most productive. Exhaustion also delayed work. Yet, they did not give up especially when they saw Tariq leading them relentlessly and working even harder than they were.

They pushed themselves beyond their limits every day. At the end of the day, the volunteers would sit around a campfire and while they had their dinner, Tariq would teach them all he had learned from his favorite professor at the university at Aqlab. They enjoyed this part as they devoured the information. He would repeat the lessons every day so that they could remember them better. The planning for the next day's activities would also happen around the campfire. Then, all would retire for the night. Thus, went an entire week at the hospice; cleaning, scrubbing, tending wounds, nurturing the sick and learning new things about nursing and medical care.

There were five deaths during this week and all were beyond help. The first death of a young soldier just a few years older than Tariq nearly broke him. The wound was deep and the infection had spread all over and there was little anyone could do except try and keep him and his area clean. Everyone knew the end was nearing including the poor soldier, but there was no sense of morbidity in the air.

The soldier beckoned Tariq the day before he died and said, "I wish I could stand up and salute you, sir. You are no less than the hero of all of these wars. You are also fighting a battle and your battle is nobler than the other battle I fought in because there, I killed living people and here, you are trying to save dying people. We need more Crusades like yours, sir." Thus saying, he raised his hand in a salute even as he was lying down. "I am not sad to die, sir, especially now when I have seen the work of good people like you. I know I will die a painless and peaceful death. Thank you again, sir."

This was the third day. On the fourth day, this soldier and three others like him passed away. And on the sixth day, one more passed away. Each of the five soldiers was given a respectful burial in a graveyard that existed besides the building. For the first time, the remaining soldiers did not feel the fear of death when they saw their comrades dying. The sight of this noble medicine man seemed to give them courage. In fact, many of them became so physically fit and mentally alert in a couple of days that they offered their voluntary services as well and the number of volunteers increased to 15 and the unrelenting work continued.

At the end of the week, Tariq invited Captain Philip to visit the hospice. The captain was very busy with other activities and refused initially saying that he would come another day. But Tariq insisted saying, "The people there have been working very hard and a word of appreciation from their commander-in-chief would make them very happy."

So, Captain Philip agreed to come. But, he said, "I will come only if you let me bring some guests with me to your hospice." Tariq was thrilled to hear the captain say "your hospice" and he loved the sense of ownership that he felt with the place. He said, "I would love to introduce my volunteers to other people. They have seen few human beings other than the dead and dying ones. They will be happy to welcome healthy guests in their midst."

As he completed these words, the curtain that closed another segment in the tent opened and from the doorway walked his parents and his sister. He was amazed and thrilled too. He ran towards them and hugged them. The awkwardness of what happened in their house previously seemed to have vanished into thin air. It was a moment of pure happiness to see her husband and son bond without any more feeling of rancor.

"How did you know where to find me?"

Everyone turned to look at Imelda who was worried that Tariq may be angry for not listening to him when he said that he wanted to go without telling his parents. But now when she saw Tariq with his father, she knew that she had done the right thing. It would have been unforgivably cruel to have come away without telling Haroun and Gabe. They would have died from the agony of separation. They didn't deserve that.

Tariq looked at her and thanked her silently and said, "I was so wrong, father. I now realize the realities and pain of the outside world. There were so many times when things did not go the way I wanted the last few days and for sometime a murderous rage overtook me. I needed to summon all my willpower to stop myself from doing terrible things. When that soldier died and I realized my helplessness, I was overcome with rage. Yet, I could do nothing."

He continued as his parents looked on lovingly, "And I felt this helpless rage despite being brought up in luxury and not knowing what hatred was until I reached here. All the love you gave me was not sufficient to balance that rage. It had to come out and I had to deal with it. And father, you have had such a difficult childhood and one look of love from mother was enough to change all that hate to love. I have had such an easy and loving life and yet all the love in my life was not enough to stop the hate. I am sorry for the cruel words, father. I do not know how I will redeem myself for what I said to you."

Haroun simply came over to his son and hugged him tightly, "No matter what you say, you are my son and my love for you will never fade. Now, let us go see this hospice care."

# *Chapter 10*
## LORD RALPH AND LADY GRISELDA COME TO CAPTAIN PHILIP'S CAMP

Lord Ralph was devastated when he heard of his daughter's disappearance and he feared the worst. He loved his daughter and found so many qualities of Gabriella in her; her ability to be unconventional without compunction, and her strength to stand on her principles. Imelda was specifically antagonistic towards her mother, Lady Griselda, who she believed was using the Crusades to achieve her own ends.

Lady Griselda was as ambitious as she was weak. She used everyone else to do her bidding. Getting married into the Gascoigne family strengthened her ambitious streak and she now wanted control of Mordo too. Mordo was her parent's home and Gascoigne was a vassal state of Mordo. Lady Griselda's ambition was to reverse roles and make Mordo a vassal state of Gascoigne.

To this end, she was hoping to get her daughter married to a powerful Duke in Castile who was a close cousin of the King of Andalusia. She was dreaming of becoming one of the most powerful royal ladies in all of Andalusia. When she heard of Imelda's disappearance, she thought it was the end of her personal dreams!

Lord Ralph and Lady Griselda decided to travel to Captain Philip's camp to find out more. When they reached the camp, they were delighted to hear that Imelda had returned safely. When they heard about Tariq, Lord Ralph was overjoyed. He was so happy that his dear cousin, Gabriella had done so well for herself. He was happy to hear about Haroun as well. It made him so happy that love could change a person so much for the better. He wished he could have done the same magic on his wife who was so obsessed with power and wealth that she was willing to sacrifice the happiness of her daughter also.

When Lady Griselda heard of Tariq, she was livid with fury. Even as girls growing up together in the large Castle of Mordo, she hated her cousin, Gabriella, because of the excessive love and affection showered on her by everyone. She was always relegated to somewhere in the lower rungs of the hierarchical order. She refused to see the bravery and valor of Gabriella and instead, simply chose to be jealous of her right through.

She was so happy that Gabriella had chosen to run away with the Moor which allowed her to marry Ralph and become the Lady of Gascoigne. If

Gabriella had stayed on at Mordo, she would have been married off to someone much lower in rank. And now, Griselda thought, the entire family was back to creating problems for her. She would have none of it, she decided. There is no way she would allow her daughter to be married off to some unknown 'medicine man' with no political clout.

She knew that her husband would not support her in this regard and she had to do something before things went out of hand. Griselda may not have been good at heart but she was shrewd and sharp of mind. She thought out a plan and sent word for a paid assassin who she knew was part of Captain Philip's army.

"Kill Tariq and announce that you did it because you were the child of one of the men that Haroun had killed during his days as a paid assassin. Tell everyone present that you recognized Haroun and wanted revenge. You wanted Haroun to live and suffer the pain of losing someone he loved just like you did. That's why you killed Tariq instead of Haroun. I will compensate you for your work. Set the price and I will pay you."

The assassin was more than happy to do his lady's bidding. He did not want money from Lady Griselda. He had already done work for her previously and was aware of her ambitions. He said, "When your daughter marries the Duke of Castile, you must promise to get me a high position in the army." Lady Griselda readily agreed. After all, it would do her good to have men from her side in high positions in the army of Castile. So, it was agreed that the assassin would find the opportune moment and kill Tariq and make the announcement.

The proclamation of revenge was also important for Lady Griselda. She wanted the entire family of Gabriella broken and shattered. The son killed for revenge, the father broken by guilt for having been responsible for his son's death, and the mother devastated by the sight of her dead son!

All of them set out to the hospice, the assassin following at a safe distance behind the Gascoigne party. When they reached the hospice, everyone was amazed at the sight of the place. No one had ever seen a hospital so impeccably clean and wonderfully maintained. Everyone would run at the sight of sick and wounded people except, perhaps, those who loved them the most. Here, however, the sick and wounded looked happy and rested. Tariq had created magic and all it needed was determination, hard work, and an innate ability for compassionate leadership.

They met the Mordo party in the beautiful lawns of the new hospice. Gabriella was thrilled to see her cousin. She had long forgiven him for what he did when he was young. The family reunion was happy and greatly emotional. It was getting dark and suddenly, from the darkest corner of the lawn, someone came charging at Tariq and before Tariq could react, he saw his father in front of him and a deadly serrated knife plunged halfway into his stomach. Shocked but getting his wits back in an instant, he caught the man with the knife and pinned him down. The other volunteers came running and held the man down while Tariq ran towards his wounded father. Everyone was in shock as they saw Haroun breathing heavily and bleeding even more heavily with the knife still in his abdomen.

# *Conclusion*

Smiling weakly, Haroun spoke to Tariq, "I suppose I have not yet forgotten the tricks of my old profession. I am happy that they came of use to save my son and redeem me of my murderous sins. You were right, Tariq. It was a miracle that your mother's love made me give up my old ways and bring two beautiful children into this world. But, there is no way I could not have repented for my sins. And this, my son, is my repentance."

"I saw that man heading towards you to kill you and came just in time to save you, my beloved son. I am so happy that destiny allowed me to redeem my sins by letting me sacrifice my life for you, Tariq. I would have wanted nothing less. Look after your mother and sister. Continue the good work you are doing. Forgive the man who tried to kill you."

He looked lovingly at his grief-stricken wife and daughter and beckoned them to come closer. He hugged his beautiful family and breathed his last in peace and happiness knowing in the depths of his heart that his son had forgiven him and he was also able to get redemption.

The others were stunned to speechlessness. They merely watched the entire scene unfold. Lady Griselda shuddered at the failure of her plan. But, she had to wait for another opportune time. She was confident that the assassin will never sacrifice her identity. He needed her to get his sentence reduced or completely waived. She held the political clout to do that.

The assassin repeated what was taught to him by Lady Griselda and told everyone that he had actually come to kill Tariq to extract revenge from Haroun who had killed his father more than 25 years ago. He wanted Haroun to suffer the pain he suffered when he lost his father. But, somehow, Haroun saw him coming and came between the knife and his son and became the victim instead.

Although Griselda was not as happy as she would have been had her original plan of killing Tariq happened, seeing the devastated expression on Gabriella's face gave her some amount of satisfaction. She would still wait for another time to kill Tariq. For now, she will have to keep up the pretense of feeling sorry for the death of her cousin's dear beloved husband.

Inside her mind though, she was beginning to work out the next plan to target Tariq and get him out of his daughter's life. Imelda was born to build her dreams not to marry some unknown 'medicine man."

Tariq, Gabriella and Ayesha sat around Haroun and gave in shamelessly to their grief. The thought of never being able to see his father again tore at Tariq's heart. The cruel words he used to hurt his father recently hurt him so much now that he thought his heart would break. If only he had been patient and waited for the anger against his father to die down. His father would have been alive today. He was no worse than an assassin, he thought. At least the assassin knew what he was getting into and took responsibility for his actions. Here, his father paid for his mistakes and took on the onus of his problems and his inability to handle things with maturity.

He somehow sensed that this was not the end. There was more pain waiting for him. He should never have left his beloved Aqlab. Would he ever get back home?

REINA DONOVAN

# THE MOOR

## Book III of the Crusader Trilogy

before attempting any techniques outlined in this book.

By reading this document, the reader agrees that under no circumstances are is the author responsible for any losses, direct or indirect, which are incurred as a result of the use of information contained within this document, including, but not limited to, — errors, omissions, or inaccuracies.

# *Introduction*

He woke up suddenly in the middle of the night, sweating profusely and his heart beating at a sickeningly fast speed! It took him a couple of minutes to realize that he was safely lying in his bed in his sleeping quarters and it was the same set of nightmares that had been waking him every night for the last six months.

The first time Tariq had this nightmare, he realized that he had woke up screaming agonizingly and had to be consoled by his mother and his fiancé. As time passed, the nightmares became so frequent that he simply accepted them as part of his nightly regimen. He had discussed the nightmares with his mother and fiancé and they both did their best to tell him not to worry much about things he was not responsible for.

He knew what they said made sense. How could the events that happened in his father's younger days be held against the son now? He was not even born when his father did what he did! And yet, he couldn't put the negative thoughts out of his mind and these recurring nightmares didn't help to allay the fears of his father's past catching up with him.

Before his father, Haroun, met his mother, Gabriella of the famed Mordo family, he worked as a paid assassin, killing for money. After he fell in love with Gabriella, Haroun gave up his ways and the couple built a beautiful home in Aqlab, a community that provided a safe haven for people like his parents, a Moor marrying a Christian. The times were not conducive for such marriages as the ongoing Crusades contributed to driving deep wedges between people of different religions.

However, free from the scourge of these wars, Haroun and Gabriella had a wonderful family in the safe environs of Aqlab. He and his sister made up the rest of the peace-loving and extremely happy family in Aqlab. By another twist of fate which resulted in a father-son misunderstanding, Tariq left home and helped refurbish old and derelict hospice care buildings run for soldiers of the Crusade Wars managed by the Order of Malta.

Just when Tariq realized the part his immature behavior played in increasing misunderstandings with his father, another tragedy occurred in which his father sacrificed his life to save his beloved son. The murderer had actually come to kill Tariq so that Haroun would know what it was like to lose a loved one and live with the pain of the loss eating into him every day of his life. But, Haroun sensed the impending danger and came between the murderer and his son and was fatally wounded by the knife meant for his son.

After that incident, Tariq's state of mind never achieved stability. Added to the pain of losing his father in such a tragic way, the idea sown by the murderer's confession of exacting revenge grew into a gigantic tree that refused to leave Tariq alone. He kept getting nightmares that people affected by his father's acts as an assassin were returning to harm him and his family. There seemed to be no escape from these thoughts!

# *Chapter 1*
## AFTER HAROUN'S DEATH

After Haroun's tragic death, Gabriella and Ayesha went back to Aqlab. They tried hard to persuade Tariq to return home with them. But he refused, saying, "I have already committed many mistakes because of my immaturity. I am responsible for father's death. If I had just given him time and been patient with him while he tried to explain things to me, he would not have died. I foolishly left home in search of redemption when there was no need to look for it. But, now I need to redeem myself for what I did to my father. I am staying on here and will be part of the hospice care. I find peace in healing. Until I find complete peace, I cannot return home, Mother."

His mother understood his dilemma and left for her home in Aqlab along with her daughter, Ayesha. Although she dreaded going back to a house in which she would never see her husband's smiling face, Gabriella felt at peace. She believed Haroun was in a better place and when he died, he perhaps felt redeemed of all his sins. So, she chose to bear the burden of her loss only in her own heart and decided to live to help her children become better people.

Tariq promised his mother that he would come to visit her soon.

With heavy hearts and a horse without a rider (Gabriella insisted on taking Haroun's favorite horse back home to Aqlab), the mother and daughter rode back home with a team of soldiers from Captain Philip's army for protection until they reached Aqlab safely. Her cousin Ralph, the king of Gascoigne, accompanied them and from there went back to his kingdom. The soldiers returned after about a week and told Tariq that his mother and sister were safe and sound at home.

Tariq flung himself into work at the hospice care. More volunteers joined his team and news of the effectiveness of his work reached far and wide. Other knights of the Order of Malta located in different areas of Andalusia called him to repeat what he did at Captain Philip's army camp. Tariq sent for two of his best friends from Aqlab who were keen on joining him in his work. They were Arthur and Carleton. During their study days, the three of them were always taking extra classes and reading up material from the library at Aqlab in medical care. They were a huge help to Tariq.

So, while Arthur and Carleton stayed back with Captain Philip's army to manage the hospice care there, he and Imelda, his fiancée (who never left his side since the day they laid eyes on each other at Aqlab) traveled from camp to camp setting up excellent hospice care facilities taking the help of local volunteers. The number of volunteers swelled so much now that they could choose the best available. They taught the volunteers all that they knew about medical care and after ensuring the camp's volunteers could manage the work on their own, Tariq and Imelda moved on to the next camp.

The War of the Crusades ensured that there was no dearth of military presence as more and more Christian soldiers were being exhorted by His Holiness, the Pope, to join the cause. On the other side, the Moor leaders were driving their men too. Although Tariq himself did not believe in the cause of the Crusades, he did not prevent other people from following their beliefs. In his training classes, he would always include a small session on the importance of peace and the horrors of war and this was the only thing he did to deter people from participating in battles and wars. But, the spirit of the crusades was so powerful that these small efforts had hardly any results as soldiers surged into the Crusade camps to participate in what they believed was a noble cause.

The presence of Imelda from the prestigious Gascoigne family helped Tariq in being accepted as part of the Christian clan although he was now getting requests to set up this kind of hospice care facility from the people fighting on the side of the Moors also. Since he was already very busy here, he had to say no to requests from the Moors for the time being.

In addition to the presence of Imelda, Tariq's demeanor and behavior were so noble and his generosity of heart and the care and concern in his eyes for the sick helped him get close to everyone in the camps he visited. He became a popular figure in all the Crusade Camps and his fame as "The Healer" spread far and wide. He was greeted with open arms wherever he went and was accepted into the fold as if he was a brother to everyone.

Imelda's love for him only grew each day as she witnessed the miracle of his caring and loving nature embrace every human being he came in contact with. Tariq loved Imelda too but the sudden tragic death of his father prevented him from thinking about marriage as yet and she was more than willing to wait until he overcame the pain and guilt he was feeling.

"I only insist that you let me come with you wherever you go so that I can help you in your endeavor to bring succor to the wounded and the sick," said Imelda when Tariq told her of his emotional dilemma and his inability to take on the responsibility of a family for the moment.

Imelda's ambitious mother, Lady Griselda, was delighted to know that the engagement of her daughter to Tariq was not to happen too soon. Although her initial plans of getting Tariq killed so that the threat of his hold over Imelda would disappear forever backfired by Haroun coming between the assassin she had hired for this job and Tariq, she was happy for the respite from the tragedy which she intended to use to find other means to get Tariq killed. There was no way she was allowing a 'mere healer' to marry her beautiful daughter. She had plans to use her daughter to enhance her own political powers by getting her married to the Duke of Castile.

Imelda was unaware of her mother's evil designs and did not even know that it was her mother's scheme to get Tariq murdered which was the reason behind Haroun's death. She knew her mother was ambitious but she had no idea that Lady Griselda would fall to such depths to achieve her selfish ends.

The assassin who had tried to kill Tariq was named Algernon and he worked as a soldier in Captain Philip's army. He claimed that the reason he came to kill Tariq was because he was the son of one of Haroun's victims during his assassin days and when he saw Haroun, he wanted to exact revenge.

When Captain Philip wanted to sentence Algernon to death for the murder of Haroun, Tariq chose to forgive him. In fact, that was the last request of his father just before his last breath. Haroun said, "Forgive the man who killed me. He has actually helped me redeem myself. Do not exact revenge from him."

In deference to his father's last wishes, he chose not to press charges and, in fact, employed him as his personal valet in the hope of converting him to becoming a better person. The rest of the people were shocked when he announced this decision. Tariq said, "My father wanted me to forgive him and I want to go one step further and give Algernon an opportunity to redeem himself. Being my personal valet will entail that he travels with me all over and help me treat the sick and wounded. Maybe, he will find redemption the same way I wanted to redeem myself when I chose to do this service."

Algernon was stunned and moved to tears. He had never heard of forgiveness until then in his lifetime. For Algernon, the concept of forgiveness remained only in the pages of the holy books; for the first time, he met a man who was willing to forgive. He was a changed man immediately. But, he was also very wary of Lady Griselda, the powerful Gascoigne lady who had recruited him to kill Tariq. He knew her well enough to realize that she would not stop at this one attempt. She will continue to look for opportunities to kill Tariq.

So, Algernon decided he would stay by the side of his new and noble master always to keep him safe. Yet, he had to pretend that he was on the side of Lady Griselda. Otherwise, she would have got him killed too and recruited another assassin to do his work. So, he chose to pretend to be on Lady Griselda's side to help her find ways to kill his master but remained by his master to ensure that not a hair on his body will be harmed.

# *Chapter 2*
# THE NIGHTMARES

Tariq's nightmares continued unabated. There were four of them that kept recurring at regular intervals. In each of the nocturnal mind journeys, Tariq was attacked in different ways and every one of the attackers claimed to be victims of his father's deeds and to have come back to exact revenge for the pain they had to endure.

The first nightmare started when Tariq awoke clutching his throat and making agonizing sounds. He realized it was only in his dreams when his mother came rushing into the room frightened by the sounds he made and shook him awake. When he came to his senses, he tried to recall what the nightmare was about and why he woke up clutching his throat feeling a dream-like sense of agony.

But, nothing came to mind. His mother had panicked but became calm when she realized that Tariq was only reacting to a bad dream. She stayed with him for a little while longer and when he slipped back into deep sleep, Gabriella quietly went back to her room. This was about a week after Haroun's death and all the funeral rituals had been completed. Captain Philip had given them some tents within the camp to stay as long as they wished. But for Gabriella, the call of her home in Aqlab was too powerful to ignore and she left with her daughter within a couple of days after that.

A few days after his mother left for Aqlab, Tariq had the nightmare again. Again, he woke up clutching his throat and screaming in agony. This time Algernon, who had a small bed in the same tent as Tariq, came rushing to his master and shook him awake, consoled him, and both went back to sleep a little while later.

Unlike the previous time, when he came to his senses, the second time he had this nightmare, Tariq could recall some parts of it and related the details to Imelda the next morning, "I remember putting something in my mouth and in a few minutes, I felt a stinging sensation in my throat as I found it difficult to take in air and I was gasping for breath and my hands automatically clutched my throat. I must have repeated the action in the dream and woke up in shock screaming without thinking about it."

Imelda placed a comforting hand on his shoulder and said, "Tariq, you must strive to put the past behind you. You are not responsible for anything that your father did. He himself died feeling peaceful and redeemed. And he has even told you to forgive

Algernon. Although you have kept him as your personal valet, I do not trust him. You have to take care of yourself. He could find a good opportunity to complete the job he had come for. If you believe that the events of the past are catching up, he will be emboldened to try new ways to achieve his 'baseless' revenge. Get yourself together, Tariq. You are doing so much of good work amidst such a chaotic war. You are trying to spread peace as much as you can. You have a heart of gold; the Lord above will take care of you. And no one can harm you."

Tariq smiled at her and said lovingly, "Thank you so much for being with me despite my inhibitions and uncertain feelings. Yes, I know I am not responsible for what has happened before me and yes, I am happy that my father died a peaceful man. Yet, my heart does quiver with fear and I can't help but see the river of blood in my father's past and can't help but hear the tortured and agonized screams of many young children who were orphaned because of what my father did. I have forgiven my father. My dear, I have even managed to overcome the sense of guilt I felt for calling my father to his death. But, I am unable to put these dreadful thoughts out of my head."

He continued, "Will you promise to stay my side until the very end?"

Imelda looked lovingly at the man she had given her heart to and said, "Nothing in this world will make me leave your side, Tariq. I was wedded to you when I gave you my heart. The wedding ceremony will only be a formal ritual for the world to see that we are husband and wife. I will always be by your side."

This calmed Tariq down and he felt so much better for Imelda's love. They went on with the day's work as they helped sick patients, cleaned wounds and helped new patients with their bedding and settling down. They supervised the cooking area and ensured hygiene rules were followed strictly. Now, that there was no dearth of volunteers, work happened at a much faster rate than before and all tasks were efficiently carried out. Medicines were stocked regularly. Quicklime was regularly mixed with water in the correct proportion to keep the hospital area disinfected always.

The days went very happily for Tariq as he, Imelda and Algernon, who now never left Tariq's side, were kept busy with work. However, Tariq dreaded the night times. The nightmares recurred and now he was seeing himself killed in numerous ways. The poisoning was the first. After a couple of weeks, he dreamt that he was shot in the back with an arrow smeared with the poison of nightshade. He was screaming in pain and tried in vain to pull out the poisoned spear. There was no one to help him either. The pain of death did not worry him as much as the feeling of desolation and loneliness he felt when these nightmares came to haunt him.

In another one, he was riding alone in a dense jungle and suddenly, the earth under his feet gave way and he found himself in a deep ditch with no way to escape. He saw himself dying from starvation and thirst. In his last moments, he saw the horrifying laughter of a stranger who looked down on him and told him, "Now you must know the pain of loneliness I felt when your father killed my father for money." The man threw down some gold coins and said, "Here, take this money and give it to your father when you meet him in hell and tell him this money is his reward for having his son killed."

The first time Tariq had this dream, he thought he would simply take a dagger and plunge it into himself. He just couldn't bear the mental torture of this entire emotion of revenge.

In the worst of the nightmares, he saw his home at Aqlab engulfed in a raging fire and he was trapped inside with his mother and sister. All three of them were trying to scream for help but no sound was coming from their throats. And they felt the fire singe into their skin, they saw hazy faces of men looking down from above laughing with sadistic pleasure at their fiery plight. This was the worst nightmare Tariq had. In fact, he did not even discuss this with Imelda. He did talk about the other three nightmares that were torturing him. He couldn't bring himself to talk about his mother's and sister's deaths to Imelda. He simply bore the agony of the nightmare and mental torture alone.

It was over six months now since his father was killed and Algernon became a true friend. He never left his side and was always there to do things for him. He helped him in the hospice work. He got him his food. He did everything a valet would do for him and his presence became comforting for Tariq. And when they were out in the open, Algernon behaved like his personal bodyguard not allowing any strangers to go near him without checking their true intentions. His eyes were constantly darting back and forth as if he expected some danger to befall his master. Even Imelda noted this. While Imelda didn't trust him fully, Tariq liked having Algernon around. However, he did not discuss his nightmares with anyone else but Imelda.

There was an almost unsaid understanding between Algernon and Tariq that neither of them would discuss the circumstance of his father's death. Yet, when they were alone in the room, there were many times when Tariq thought that Algernon started to say something but ended up keeping quiet.

In fact, Tariq once said to him, "Do you wish to say something, Algernon?"

When he heard the question, Algernon almost steeled himself to say something but a deeply embedded instinct prevented him from telling Tariq about his prospective mother-in-law and her murderous intentions. He somehow felt he needed to pretend to be on her side to keep his master safe. His master would never allow him to continue putting up a façade for his sake and if they confronted Lady Griselda, nothing would come of it because nobody will believe Algernon.

On the contrary, he might be put to death for trying to defame the Gascoigne family and Lady Griselda could use one of her other cronies to harm Tariq. He couldn't let that happen! So, he kept quiet and bore his own agony alone in the same way as his master was putting up with the agony of his nightmares and the devilish games that his poor mind was playing on him.

Yes, he was never far away from Tariq and so, even when he and Imelda thought they were alone and discussed the dreams in detail, Algernon was hovering unseen and heard every bit of it. No one knew this except Algernon himself and his heart bled for his master. But, he could do nothing except pray to the Lord Almighty and ask Him to take these satanic thoughts away from his master's mind.

However, he did not realize at that time that these dreams would actually help him in bringing to light Lady Griselda's misdeeds to the forefront! That idea came later.

# *Chapter 3*
## LADY GRISELDA BEGINS HER PLOTTING

L ady Griselda was talking to Algernon in secrecy. Only the two of them were present and she was sounding very impatient. Her daughter refused to leave Tariq alone and come back to Gascoigne with her. Her love for Tariq seemed to be growing faster than Griselda's resentment to the presence of the mere medical man in her daughter's life.

Although her first attempt to rid the entire family of Haroun from her daughter's life backfired on her, she was happy that at least one of them was dead even though he was the not the intended victim. But, one thing about Griselda was her ability to pick up the thread and continue her quest without getting too perturbed by small problems.

So, Haroun died instead of Tariq. She had planned to get Tariq killed and let the rest of the family go back to Aqlab and die of heartbreak. But, however, the father came between the assassin and his son and sacrificed himself. When she first saw the fallen

163

Haroun, Griselda panicked that her true intentions would come out. But, then the assassin had stuck to the idea she had told him about and thought he would become imprisoned by Captain Philip.

But, a miracle happened instead. Tariq had chosen to forgive the man she had hired to kill him. In fact, he had made Algernon, the assassin, his personal bodyguard hoping to change his attitude from taking a life to protecting a life. At first, Griselda worried that Algernon might confess everything. But, later she realized that he knew and feared her power and would not want to antagonize her. Moreover, who would believe a mere soldier?

Hence, she turned tables and chose to continue to use Algernon's service to find a convenient way of getting rid of Tariq without any connection to her. She wanted her daughter to believe in her because without her daughter's consent, she will not be able to achieve any of her dreams.

Until now, Griselda was being patient with Algernon as he claimed to be working on ideas that would help her get what she needed without arousing any suspicion.

"You will have to give me some time, Lady Griselda," Algernon had told her a month after he became Tariq's bodyguard. "I will have to first win his trust and only then will he allow me to get close to him. Moreover, your daughter does not trust me at all. Give me some time and I will find a way."

What she did not know was that Algernon was a changed man and he was staying as close to Tariq as possible to save him from danger. He was only using the ruse of time to let Griselda continue to believe that he was on her side. But, today, she was livid. She had sent word through a trusted servant to get him to meet her in the woods surrounding Captain Philip's camp after dark.

She was glaring at him and now and was telling him, "Algernon, it has been more than 6 months since you have been with Tariq. I have been hearing a lot of news that Tariq has become very close to you. Even my daughter told me today that maybe you are a changed man and you seem to have no intention of harming Tariq. This has got me worried. Are you really a changed man after Tariq's act of forgiveness? I am quite certain you know the consequences of turning against me, Algernon. I will make sure you are tried and killed for some treacherous act! You know the powers I wield in Castile. Now, tell me the truth."

Algernon maintained a calm demeanor and told her, "Lady Griselda, you are suspecting me needlessly. I am on your side. You think I am going to be happy with being a personal bodyguard for a medical man who has no royal support and who has only the love and affection of hundreds of soldiers he has cured and treated? No, Lady Griselda! I want to be in a high position of power and I am certain that you will give me my reward for helping you get rid of Tariq and after your daughter gets married to the Duke."

Griselda appeared consoled by Algernon's speech. But she was impatient as well.

"You don't understand my haste. I need Tariq out of the way faster. I need Imelda to be introduced to the Duke soon so that he falls for her and marries her. Her beauty has already reached his ears but so has this horrifying tale of an impending engagement with Tariq. He is getting impatient to marry her but she is behaving stubbornly, refusing to leave Tariq's side."

"And my husband is siding with his uncle, the King of Mordo, and does not have any intention of becoming more powerful. Let us offer the soldiers who are fighting the Holy War food and accommodation while they travel through Gascoigne and that would be like fighting the War itself, he says. Mordo is getting the attention of the Duke for sending a great number of soldiers to the War and it looks like Uncle Esmour will get more land and soldiers! I need Tariq dead soon. Otherwise, I am doomed and if I am doomed so are you."

Algernon realized from this impassioned speech that he needed to tune up his act a little more to make his master safe and keep the pretense real for Lady Griselda. Suddenly, a plan struck him in his head. As his own plan evolved in his mind, he told Lady Griselda of a parallel plan of how he intended to get Tariq killed. He told her about the dreams that Tariq had been having and he was thinking that if he recreated a nightmare and Tariq dies, he will not blame anyone and simply think that fate has found a way for retribution.

"He has been talking to your daughter about this as well. I could recreate it so that she will also believe that fate has done what has to be done. You will be able to get rid of Tariq and your daughter might also simply accept the inevitable and move on with her life according to the plans you have laid out for her."

Lady Griselda's eyes brightened at this. She felt happy that she had trusted Algernon and waited patiently for him to get the right opportunity. Today, she realized that the perfect opportunity had come and Algernon had lived up to her expectations. She promised herself that she would definitely reward him with a high position. She needed such resourceful men in high positions anyway.

Imelda had not spoken to Griselda about Tariq's nightmares. But that was not expected because she had never failed to show her contempt towards her daughter's choice of men. She needed to change her attitude towards Tariq temporarily. This would endear her to Imelda and when Algernon's plan succeeded, no one will find any reason to suspect her. In fact, as per Algernon's first plan, no one would even know who was responsible for Tariq's death. Also, she needed to know about those nightmares so that she could verify Algernon's story.

But, for the moment, she was delighted with the outcome of her meeting with Algernon. He had surpassed her expectations and now she simply had to be patient and wait for the plan to be put into action and watch Imelda freed from the clutches of the Healer!

# *Chapter 4*
# THE POISON

Algernon was not very happy with the outcome of the meeting with Lady Griselda. He saw her impatience as a sign of desperation and unless he did something soon, his master's life would be in danger. He had told Lady Griselda that he would recreate one of the nightmares of Tariq and he had chosen the first one, the one where Tariq wakes up clutching his throat as the searing pain of the swallowed poison affected him.

Now, he had to work out a plan wherein Tariq would appear to get poisoned but he would be safe as well. He was not sure how to work this out but he needed to put this plan into action so that Griselda would give him some more time to work on another scheme, which would not fail. She would not know that Algernon was behind the plot of saving his master as well.

As he was thinking these thoughts and walking back to the camp, he saw the weeds of serpent windroot growing all over the dense woods. And a great plan

169

struck his mind by which he would poison his master, save him from dying, and convince him to go back to Aqlab, his home, far away from danger.

Before all this, he did think of approaching Imelda for help by revealing the truth of her mother's intentions. But, he discarded that idea immediately since she still doubted the change of his personality. He was hurt by her doubt initially. He thought if she was willing to believe that Haroun could turn over a new leaf overnight for the sake of his love, how could she not believe that he had chosen to walk the right path driven by his compassion of Tariq? Was her faith in love stronger than her faith in Tariq's forgiving and compassionate nature? He found it strange but he chose to bear this manfully because his only intent was to keep Tariq safe from the clutches of the wicked woman, Griselda.

A week after the meeting with Griselda, Algernon was ready with the plan. It was a dark night and all the volunteers from the hospice care were sitting around a cozy campfire having their evening meal. Tariq, Imelda and Algernon were there too and the food was being passed around. As always, when it came to Tariq, Algernon reached out for the plate and served his master. The main meat dish was accompanied with a beautiful looking salad with some greens, flowers and sprinkled with olive oil and herbs.

As Algernon served the salad, he surreptitiously mixed something with his master's salad and also mixed it with the main serving dish. He then went around and ensured that everybody had a little bit of the food he had tampered with. He made sure he also ate some of it. After the meal, as usual, they cleared up the food and sat around for the class that Tariq took. Today, he was discussing the different kinds of ointments that could be made with herbs and plants growing in the dense jungle.

Suddenly, Tariq stood up from his place clutching his throat and, for a moment, Imelda thought he was having the nightmare while he was awaking. Then she, along with everyone else, realized that he was actually struggling to breathe and before anyone could react, he fell to the ground as if fainting. Imelda watched in horror as she actually saw the nightmare that Tariq had described to her quickly becoming a reality.

She rushed to Tariq and everyone helped him to his feet and took him inside the hospital and laid him on a clean bed. Imelda realized Tariq had only fainted and yet, his breath was coming in short bursts and he was looked pale. She looked at Algernon for help and found him sick with worry. He looked around at all the other people and everyone looked fearful and scared wondering what happened to their beloved healer.

They washed his face, made him comfortable, and watched over him the entire night. This was what he had taught them to do. If there was a wound, then they could have cleaned it. But, there was no such thing and all they could do was to wait for something to happen. In about one hour, a lot of volunteers began to feel nauseous too and started vomiting. Except for two of the volunteers and Imelda, everyone else including Algernon fell sick though none fainted like Tariq had done. They merely vomited their dinners and, after some rest, they felt fine and normal.

News reached Captain Philip and everyone from the camp came to visit the sick people especially Tariq. Lady Griselda was also there and though her face showed sympathy and sadness, she was delighted to see the results of Algernon's brilliant plan take such great shape. Seeing so many people being sick, everyone decided that something wrong with the food and that is why everyone fell ill.

Imelda realized it must have been something in the salad because the three people who were not affected by nausea did not eat the salad. Nothing was left over and hence nobody could examine the contents. Lady Griselda thought the plan was outstanding. Tariq would die. Her daughter would think life played a cruel trick and simply made his nightmares a reality through a strange twist of fate. After a few days of mourning, she would be back to her cheery self and as Tariq was not there to hold her back, she would return home to Gascoigne and Imelda will be able to put her plan into action.

Imelda's mind was still fuzzy. How could the nightmare have turned out to be true? Did divine retribution really exist? How could a dream be realized so perfectly? Now, thinking about it, every detail of the scene of Tariq's nightmare matched with what had happened yesterday evening. She remembered the details vividly because Tariq had spoken about it numerous times.

She remembered so well that he had said in his dream, he was sitting in one of the evening camps with the volunteers. He had said that suddenly in the middle of the conversation, he felt a searing pain in his throat and he woke up from the nightmare holding his throat and sweating profusely. This was exactly what had happened yesterday too. "How could this be?"

Imelda didn't realize that she exclaimed this loudly and everyone rushed to her side worried for her well-being asking her what she was saying. Imelda came to her senses immediately and just pretended to cry that the exclamation was only a rhetorical question to the Almighty above as to how He could do this to her by wanting to take Tariq away from her. Some deeply ingrained instinct told her to hold back the information about the nightmares and just pretend like everybody else that this was a case of bad food eaten by everyone. She was sure there was more to this than what was visible to everyone else.

All the people from the camp and the hospice were praying hard for their beloved healer. It would be such a quirk of fate that a person like Tariq, who practiced and preached peace and openly spoke against war, even if it was fought in name of God, should die from being poisoned. Many more questions were being raised in the minds of the people. How come the others who had the salad were only slightly affected whereas Tariq had still not recovered from the effects? But for now, the most important thing on everybody's minds, except Lady Griselda, was the safe recovery of Tariq.

Algernon never left Tariq's side, constantly wiping his brow of sweat and keeping him cool with wads of wet cloth. The fever raged right through the night and suddenly, as if by a miracle, the fever subsided in the morning and Tariq woke up as if everything about last night was only a dream.

When he opened his eyes, the first person Tariq laid

his eyes on was Algernon. The look of concern in his eyes touched Tariq's heart and he smiled at his new friend comfortingly. Everyone else heaved a sigh of relief. In fact, there arose a cheer right through the crowd of people who were waiting anxiously outside the hospice care building for some news about Tariq. He got up from the bed and felt freshened and absolutely fine. The searing pain in his throat had disappeared completely. He looked at Imelda who was shedding tears of joy and smiled back at her.

Captain Philip thumped him on his back and said, "You are fit to be a soldier!" So saying, he went back to the camp knowing the day's tasks awaited him. The rest of the people slowly turned back to their work too and the only ones left were Tariq, Imelda, Algernon and Lady Griselda, who was trying her best to avoid showing the anger and resentment at this miraculous survival of Tariq.

"So, what actually happened, Tariq," she asked showing a pretense of concern and care. Imelda looked at her mother strangely wondering why and how her mother suddenly appeared to care for Tariq when, until a week ago, she made no bones in letting Imelda know that Tariq was not fit enough to be the King and ruler of Gascoigne.

Tariq answered respectfully, "I can only remember the pain at my throat, the fever that raged in my body, and suddenly a sense of being refreshed and rejuvenated. I don't know what happened at all." Tariq was, of course, well aware that this scene was exactly what happened in the first of his nightmares and he had the same doubts that Imelda had. They exchanged meaningful glances and knew the subject of the nightmare was best left unspoken for now.

Algernon's eyes did not miss this exchange nor did they miss the anger in Lady Griselda's eyes clearly directed at him. Of course, she had made sure that only he saw the rage in her eyes. He knew that before the next meeting with her, he needed to come up with some suitable excuse of this 'failed mission.'

For the moment, Algernon reveled in the joy of saving his master. He was trained in different methods of killing and poison was one of them. He recognized the wildly growing poisonous serpent windroot that day and he also had recognized Angel's Belladonna that was known to be a great antidote for a mild windroot poisoning. He had carefully pulled out the most tender windroot leaves where the venom was not fully developed and had mixed it with leaves of antidote, Angel's Belladonna. He knew that this combination would appear to act as a poison but in fact would clear the human system of impurities.

The physical effects were, however, sufficient for

people to think he was poisoned and he had experienced a miraculous recovery. The people he was concerned about was Lady Griselda, Imelda and Tariq himself. He wanted to gain time and trust from Lady Griselda. He wanted Imelda and Tariq to believe that his nightmares can come true and that it was in the best interest for Tariq to return home to Aqlab.

Although Algernon knew that Tariq and Imelda loved each other, he knew even more certainly that Lady Griselda would do everything in her power to prevent the marriage from happening. Algernon's other hope was that Tariq would believe so much in his nightmares being realized, he will not jeopardize Imelda's life and would insist that she move away from him and find someone else to marry and be happy.

Looking at the faces of these three people, Algernon was quite sure that today's experiment had given good results. And he had chosen to mix the entire salad (after he served Tariq) with a very mild and small dose of the concoction so that the others would also be affected but not as much as Tariq would be. By doing this, all the people would simply put the effect down to bad food being eaten by everyone. Perhaps, Tariq took a larger portion and hence was affected more adversely than the others!

# *Chapter 5*
## ALGERNON AND HIS DILEMMAS

A couple of days after the poisoning incident, Tariq felt much better and was ready to get back to work. Meanwhile, Lady Griselda sent word to Algernon for a secret meeting. Algernon met her at the appointed time and at the appointed place. Her rage was so evident at his failure that Algernon cringed under her stare. He could have easily killed her but that would not have helped him or Tariq in any way. He wanted to bring to the fore her treacherous ways or make sure his master was completely safe from her evil intentions. Moreover, she had many of her guards protecting her at all times.

"What happened, Algernon?" thundered Lady Griselda. She looked ugly when she was angry. But, Algernon stood his ground and told her, "I don't know, Lady Griselda. I did everything the way I told you I would. His system must be really strong or the prayers of the people who love him must have been answered by the Lord Almighty."

"But, do not worry, Lady Griselda. He may have escaped this time. But, he certainly fears for what the future holds for him. He is suddenly realizing the power of retribution. There are two more nightmares that plague him and I will make sure the next one does not miss out the real ending."

"What are you planning this time?" Algernon told her about the second nightmare of Tariq where someone shoots him while he is traveling alone in the dense jungle. He said, "I will find an opportunity for him to travel alone and then I will follow him and shoot him with a nightshade-tipped arrow and leave him to die in desolation just like how it happens in his nightmare."

While Griselda appeared slightly pacified with this, she warned him, "If you fail this time, you will be sorry that you ever laid eyes on my face!" With this stern warning, she walked off in a huff not before telling him that she wanted to know exactly which date he planned to attack Tariq in this manner. He promised her he would find the most opportune time and pass on the details of the day and date to her.

Algernon realized Griselda was not completely convinced of his plans and he needed to do something soon to bring her cruel intentions out in the open or work on his master plan to ensure he left Captain Philip's camp and Imelda forever and went back home to Aqlab. Although he told her of his plans, he had no intention of carrying it out that way at all. Even if it came to him having to shoot that damned arrow, he would make sure he missed again and would not hesitate to take on the wrath of Griselda rather than let his master die.

Algernon suddenly realized that the sense of peace he felt while trying to protect someone is a powerful emotion unlike the restlessness he felt when he was killing someone! He wondered why this thought of using his skills to save and protect people instead of killing them never came to his mind before he met Tariq. Was it Tariq's unconditional love or his ability to forgive such a grave crime that worked this wonder? He knew he may never know the answer. But Algernon was sure of one thing. Never would he raise his weapon to kill anyone, not even Lady Griselda!

He came back to the camp, unseen by Tariq and heard his voice pleading with Imelda. "My dear, my nightmare is coming true. You saw what happened to me! There are people out there who are trying to take revenge for my father's deeds. And there seems to be some kind of divine intervention too, don't you think? The scene was exactly how it happened when I slept."

"I was also thinking of that, Tariq. There must be

some explanation for that. Did you discuss your dream with anyone else but me?"

"No! That's why I somehow feel I am fated to end my life sooner than later. Now I want to listen to me carefully and do as I say. You must leave me and go back to Gascoigne and find someone else to marry and lead a happy life. I have no doubt that I will die very soon. Something deep inside my heart is warning me. I cannot make you happy. Leave me and go away!"

Imelda looked at Tariq with a mixture of sadness and anger. She spoke calmly though because she understood Tariq's torment. She said, "Tariq, if in your heart you feel that you are going to die, deep in my heart, I can see beautiful images of our life together in happiness and joy in Aqlab when all this is over. And, love is not some object, which I can move from one heart to another. My love has been given to you. Even if you give it back to me, I cannot take it. So, don't talk of me going away from you. I will be there right by your side all through your long life."

Tariq realized there was no point in trying to persuade Imelda. But he knew that he had to find a way to either make her leave him or to leave her. As these thoughts were going on in his mind, they heard a rustle and heard Algernon announce himself. Tariq called him in and asked, "Algernon, what do you think of the poisoning incident?"

Algernon was taken aback because he suddenly thought that maybe both of them suspected him in some way. He looked surprised and said, "You mean the food poison?"

"Yes, Algernon, if something was wrong with the salad, how come I was so badly affected and the others were not as badly affected?"

"I don't know, master Tariq. Maybe you ate a bigger portion of the salad."

"What if the poison was intended for me?"

Algernon looked surprised and said, "Why should anyone try to do that?"

The moment he asked the question, Tariq realized how foolish it sounded. He was the classic example of why anyone would want to hurt Algernon. He looked shamefacedly at Tariq and his facial expressions told Tariq and Imelda that question need not be answered.

Then, he asked, "Are you suspecting me of some foul play?"

Imelda nodded while Tariq looked doubtful. For some reason, Imelda thought this was a good time to clarify her doubts with Algernon. She said, "You did accept that you came to kill Tariq for revenge. How can we believe that you have not given up that idea yet?" Her eyes blazed just like her mother's, thought Algernon to himself. But, he knew the blaze in Imelda's eyes protected Tariq unlike the blaze in her mother's eyes.

He looked calmly at both of them and gave an answer that came from the bottom of his heart, "Yes, I came to kill Tariq. But, Tariq taught me a wonderful thing. He taught me the art of forgiveness. He taught me this by choosing to forgive me for my extremely grave sin of killing his father. If he can forgive me for killing his father, shouldn't I also do the same thing?"

He continued, "I have been with Tariq and you for over 6 months now and there were so many opportunities to take revenge if I wanted to. No, Lady, I am a changed man. I feel a deep sense of guilt for what I did in my previous life and I want to atone for it. This opportunity of protecting the healer is my way of redemption. I beg you not to doubt my intentions. I am ready to lay down my life before I let any harm befall my master."

Tariq came across and embraced Algernon. He felt so happy that the true power of forgiveness was so clearly seen in the case of Algernon. He said, "I do not doubt you anymore, dear friend. And I am not your master. I am your friend and mentor. You must forgive Imelda's doubt too because she did that because of her deep love for me."

Algernon said, "I am not angry at all with the lady. I feel happy that there is another person in your life who is ready to take on any challenge to keep her love safe!" Imelda smiled at this remark and all doubts vanished from her mind.

She bade them goodnight and went to her tent. Tariq then turned to Algernon and said, "My friend, I need your help. I somehow feel that I will not live for long. This poisoning episode has created some kind of a fear psychosis in me. I don't want Imelda to stay with me because her life would be so much happier if she chose someone from her own rank and class and settled down in life. But, she refuses to go away and so, I must go away. Let us leave right now and go on to another camp that has already sent word to mc to help them set up their hospice. Will you go with me?"

Algernon was overjoyed at this. It came about exactly the way he had intended it to happen. Although he knew that the love between his master and Imelda was deep and pure, it was the main cause of danger for Tariq's life. If Imelda was to go back to Gascoigne and Griselda was able to achieve her ambitions, then Tariq's life was of no consequence to Lady Griselda. She would leave him in peace. He immediately agreed to go with Tariq and they packed their belongings into a bundle and both left Captain Philip's camp in the dead of night.

# *Chapter 6*
## THE NIGHTSHADE-TIPPED ARROW AND THE PIT

T ariq and Algernon kept walking into the dense jungle careful not to make a noise and wake up anyone. They led their horses silently on foot until they reached a safe distance from the camp. Then, they got on horseback and rode for about a couple of hours making sure it would be impossible for anyone to know in which direction they went in. Tariq did not want to be found. He wanted to go missing until Imelda took him for dead and found happiness with someone else.

They stopped at a clearing after riding for some distance and lay down to rest. Algernon kept a watch for wild animals or any other kind of danger while Tariq slept. He thought to himself, "It is good that Tariq decided to stay away from Imelda. Unwittingly, he has realized the true cause of the problem in his life though his intentions to leave Imelda were noble and borne out of love. But, I don't trust Griselda to wait patiently for things to happen. I have to keep my master safe at least until Imelda agrees to marry the Duke."

Suddenly, he thought he heard a sound in the dense thicket. He was up and very alert, ready to tackle any danger. But, soon things became quiet again. Yet, he could have sworn he heard the sound of human breathing close by. The talents he acquired as an assassin included the deep powers of the senses. He could hear, sense and feel the presence of danger very acutely.

After three hours, he was supposed to wake Tariq and take his turn to sleep. But, now his senses were too alert to dangers to allow him to sleep. Instead, he continued to keep watch while his master slept. When Tariq awoke, the sun was already up and Algernon was wearing his jacket and hat and looked just like him.

He turned and smiled at his friend, "Why did you not wake me up for my turn of watch so you could sleep? And why are you wearing my clothes?"

Algernon smiled back and said, "I didn't feel sleepy and you needed the sleep. So, I kept watch for your turn too. And would you mind if we exchanged clothes? In fact, these clothes fit me so well and the color is better than mine."

"Of course, we can exchange our jackets. Give me yours. It is getting windy."

So, the two men exchanged and wore each other's clothes. From the back, no one would know the one in Tariq's clothes was actually Algernon. This plan materialized in his mind when he was certain that there was another human being around here somewhere. In the dark of the night, he took off his jacket and wore Tariq's. He was expecting the worst and he wanted to be ready for them!

The next morning, they freshened up at a nearby stream, ate some fruits and berries and went on their way. After riding for some time, suddenly, from out of the blue, some wild animals charged towards the two of them and in the scramble, they ended up being separated. Algernon now was convinced that Lady Griselda was planning something. All these animals would have to be gathered together by a man or men. Otherwise, they would not have attacked like this. He was scared of raising his voice to call out for Tariq because he did not want his voice to be recognized by the men. After losing the wild animals, he looked for Tariq high and low and but to no avail. He found his way back to the place they started in the morning and traced the path of the other horse.

He soon reached a clearing and there, about a couple of yards away, right in the middle of the clearing, he found a huge hole and fearing the worst, he rushed towards it. But before he could reach it, he felt a stinging pain in his back and knew he was hit. He lay low conserving his energy because he realized he had very little time to save his master. As he hid in the bushes, he saw a group of men coming towards the hole with none else but Lady Griselda!

She came to the edge of the gaping hole and looked down into it and said, "Algernon, you broke my trust. I told you if you failed this time, you would curse the day you met me. You thought I would believe your silly reasons for having missed the poisoning effect. I now know you are a changed man and you are on his side. As a punishment for your betrayal, your master dies as he dreamt of dying; being killed by the poison of nightshade and you die in the pit just like it happened in his other dream!"

So saying she rode off into the distance along with her other guards while Algernon realized what would have happened. Lady Griselda was not convinced of his plans. She must have realized that Algernon had changed sides. She knew he was too good an assassin to have missed the poisoning incident itself unless he deliberately wanted to miss it. So, she must have sent other people to follow him. Thank God, he had the idea to exchange the clothes. So, here he was waiting for the poison to kill him and there was his master lying alone and desolate in the pit actually built for him. "But, at least, he will live. I must find a way to help him up before my body gives into the effects of the poison."

Algernon slowly and patiently made his way to the pit pulling along a long sturdy vine with him. He couldn't walk anymore as the poison was spreading fast and he was becoming weak. He dragged himself the entire two yards to the pit and looked down and saw his master with his face lying downwards. No wonder that Lady Griselda did not realize that it was not Algernon but Tariq who was lying at the bottom of the pit.

But, when Tariq heard the sound of dragging, he turned and looked up to see the anguished face of his beloved friend, Algernon. Algernon threw down the vine and held on to it summoning all his strength and willpower as Tariq caught it and climbed up from the pit. When Tariq was on safe ground, Algernon left go of the vine and lay down ready to breathe his last. Tariq rushed to his friend and said, "Why did you not tell me the truth about Lady Griselda?"

"Who would have believed me, sir? And moreover, she had immense power to get me arrested and tried for some kind of treacherous deed and I would have been put to death anyway. She would have simply chosen another person to kill you. My only intention was to keep you safe from her. That is why I was so happy when you chose to leave Imelda for her own good. You had unwittingly arrived at decisions which took away the cause of danger."

He took some precious breaths and regained enough strength to lay bare his heart to his beloved master. Tariq shed copious tears as the truth behind his father's killing, the poisoning incident, now this episode was revealed to him by the dying Algernon.

"I feel at peace, Tariq. Don't mourn for me. Find your happiness. If Lady Griselda finds out you are alive, she will not stop at anything to get you killed. Go back to Aqlab and find your peace. Don't let the sacrifice of this friend of yours go in vain. Don't get yourself killed by that wicked witch!"

These were the last words Algernon said. The poison was spreading rapidly and he couldn't breathe well and, in a short while, as Tariq looked on helplessly, he saw his friend breathe his last!

# *Chapter 7*
# BACK TO MORDO

Tariq was devastated. The feeling of desolation and loneliness that kept recurring in his dreams became a reality. Here he was sitting beside his friend who had sacrificed his life for him just like his father had. Without lifting a finger, Tariq was making people who loved him die for his sake. How can he talk about peace and war and compassion? How can someone be as cruel as he was? He cried until there were no tears left in his eyes.

He got up when he felt that all the tears of life have been shed in one day. He believed that he did not cry as much even on the day his father died. At least at that time, he had his family to share his burden. Today, he was truly alone and desolate running away from people who he loved and who loved him back. He needed to stay and fight for the people he loved, not run away as he had planned to do.

But, before that, he had one important task. He needed to give a fitting burial for Algernon. He took the pickaxe that was with Algernon and he dug a grave nearby for him. He lifted him gently and carried him to the edge of the grave. Then, he climbed down into the grave and gently lifted his best friend and put him down in his final resting place. Tariq thought the tears had all dried up. But, as he lowered his friend into his grave, he felt fresh and stinging tears flow down his face. He remembered the funeral prayers that were taught to him in school and he repeated them reverently calling on the Almighty to take his friend and make sure he gets a place in heaven!

He then climbed out and filled the grave with the mud he had dug out and when the mound was raised at a good height, he sat down next to it thoroughly exhausted. He carved a cross using a carving knife he always carried around and fixed it on Algernon's grave, praying steadily for his good soul to rest in peace. By the time he finished the entire burial, it got dark and he decided to stay back until the morning. He was so exhausted emotionally and physically, that he fell asleep almost immediately.

He got up just in time to see the sun rise in the horizon and spread its orange glow all around making the entire place look beautifully golden. Tariq only wished he felt as golden inside as the world was on the outside. The one thing that stayed with Tariq other than the pain of the loss of his friend was what he said before his last breath, "Don't let my sacrifice go in vain. Don't get killed by Lady Griselda."

That sparked the idea in Tariq's mind that he should not be running away but should be embracing the loving people in his life. He ran away from his parents and his father got killed; now, he was trying to run away from his Imelda, and his best friend got killed. He decided the time for running away was over and it was time to stand and fight for his love.

Then, suddenly, he recalled the nightmare of the raging fire of his home in Aqlab and he thought of how Lady Griselda had used his nightmares to work against him. He thought it might be a great idea to catch the lady in the act this time around. He wasn't sure how to go about it though. But, a vague plan was forming in his mind.

Both their horses had strayed away somewhere and he had to walk back to Captain Philip's camp. When he was close enough to the camp, he changed his appearance to look like a sick man. When some of the soldiers in the camp saw him, they thought him to be another wounded soldier and took him to the hospice care. Once he reached the hospice, he found his old friends, Arthur and Carleton, from Aqlab and told them who he really was.

They were surprised because word had reached the place that Tariq and Algernon had gone away together and no one knew what had happened to them. Apparently, Imelda was so overcome with the fact that her beloved went away without telling her that she became lonesome and depressed. It had been over two weeks now and soldiers were sent in all directions in search of the two of them.

One set of soldiers had come back with news that they found a small mound with a cross fixed over it which looked like someone's burial place in the middle of a clearing. They found an arrow that they knew was tipped with nightshade poison and a big pit. The pit was empty, they said. No one knew what happened. But, when Imelda heard about the arrow and the pit, she had fainted and when she woke up, she wasn't the same Imelda anymore. She stopped speaking to people and roamed around calling out Tariq's name repeatedly. Just yesterday, her mother took her back to Gascoigne where she hoped she would recover her senses.

Tariq was overcome with emotion and knew he had to do something about the situation. Suddenly, he thought of his grandfather, King Esmour Martyn of Mordo that was his mother's home too. He knew that his grandfather was a powerful man and he could take his help to rein in Imelda's mother. He already knew his Uncle Ralph was there. Uncle Ralph had already met him and knew him well. In fact, after his father's death, Uncle Ralph was the one who did all the funeral arrangements and was with his mother and sister until they reached the safety of Aqlab.

With the help of his friends, he got a horse and some food and rode to Mordo. It took him two days to reach Mordo. When he saw the castle there, he was so amazed at how strikingly similar it was to his home in Aqlab. He thought of his unfortunate father who had built his wife a home just like her own home so that she never felt separated from her beloved Mordo. His resolve to bring to justice the person responsible for his father's death grew stronger.

He remained in the jungle not sure how to find his uncle or grandfather in the big castle. That's when he remembered the secret passage his mother had told him about which she and her father had used to get inside the castle. This passage led right into his grandfather's bedroom. His parents had made sure that when they told their children the truth about their previous lives, they left out no detail. He was able to recollect exactly where and how the passage could be found.

He used it to reach the other side and realized that the door was locked. He banged on it repeatedly and suddenly the door flew open and there on the other side of the threshold stood his Uncle Ralph and, behind him, an old man who looked stunned. Uncle Ralph was so happy at seeing his nephew. For King Esmour, this was like déjà vu when his daughter came through the same door more than two decades ago and everything ended in disaster.

He looked at Tariq and realized this must be his grandson. Ralph had already told him about Haroun and his daughter and the tragedy of his son-in-law's death. He paled at the thought of his daughter being alone but knew that her children will look after her well. The news of Tariq's healing powers had reached Mordo and many of the people of Mordo were eager to meet with such a noble-hearted person who chose to work with the sick and wounded instead of earning fame and power by being in the Crusades.

King Esmour was delighted at seeing his strapping and handsome grandson. They hugged and shed tears of happiness. After the initial emotions were expressed, Uncle Ralph asked him how come he was here and had entered in this way. It took Tariq some time to fill up the gaps for both his uncle and his grandfather.

While his grandfather was furious at Lady Griselda, Uncle Ralph refused to believe that his wife was capable of getting someone killed to achieve her ambitions. Then, he thought back on his own life and realized if he could have done it, maybe his wife could be capable of it too. Yet, he didn't want to give up the little bit of hope and faith he still had on his wife. They may not be the most loving couple, but he owed her the benefit of the doubt before putting a stamp of being a murderer on her.

Tariq was not angry with his uncle for his reaction and instead, said, "I agree with you, Uncle Ralph. I think Lady Griselda deserves a chance of proving her innocence. So, here is my plan." He then went on to explain to them about the nightmare where his house is set on fire and everyone inside is consigned to flames. He created a scheme around this and he felt his best friend, Algernon, would have been proud of his idea of saving his family and bringing to light the tyrannous attitude of Lady Griselda. Uncle Ralph readily agreed to the suggestion because he wanted his wife to be innocent and he thought that she would not go the heights that Tariq thought she could go to.

# *Chapter 8*
## WHAT HAPPENS IN GASCOIGNE?

Ralph left for Gascoigne immediately and King Esmour and his dear grandson left for Aqlab. Ralph reached Gascoigne and saw that his daughter was in an emotional turmoil. He reached out to her, seeing the depth of pain in her eyes, and suddenly the fact that maybe what Tariq said about his wife was true hit him.

But, he maintained his composure and asked his wife what had happened to their daughter. Why is she like this? Lady Griselda was livid though she sounded concerned for Imelda too. She told him about how Tariq had lost in mind over some nightmares of his coming true leaving him dead sooner than later. He had left Imelda for good thinking it would be better that she found another man who would live longer and keep her happier than he could.

"Doesn't it make sense to follow what Tariq says? Why can't she forget him and marry the Duke of Castile who is bewitched by her beauty? Tariq has run away from her anyway. How can a man who claims to love her run away from her?" asked Griselda of her husband.

Ralph looked at her strangely and said, 'But they do love each other very much, don't you believe that?" Griselda looked flummoxed at her husband's direct question and replied haltingly, "Yes, yes, of course. But if he has run away and he doesn't want to take the responsibility of his love, shouldn't she also forget him?"

Ralph agreed and said, "Yes, that does make sense. We will wait patiently for her to get over Tariq and then she can choose whoever she wants to marry."

"But that might be too late," Griselda bit her tongue as soon as the words were out. Ralph looked at her and said, "What do you mean by late?"

To which Griselda replied that maybe by the time she gets over Tariq, the Duke of Castile might marry someone else. "So, what! Isn't there a dearth of suitors for our beautiful girl?" Griselda simply glared at her husband and thought furiously to herself, "What sort of a man can somebody be who doesn't want more power? What kind of a man have I married? And if I hadn't stopped it, my daughter would have married a man worse than this, someone who did not even have a title!"

Ralph was talking and suddenly the word nightmares brought her back to the present. Ralph was saying to Imelda, "My dear, I know all about those nightmares. Tariq had spoken to me about it when I visited the camp occasionally. He did tell me the four nightmares he had. Do you think it is true that his dreams came true, Imelda dear?"

"I don't know what to think, father. The poisoning incident was very real and it drove Tariq insane enough to want to leave me. The scenes the soldiers described at the clearing were also starkly similar to what Tariq told me. But wait! Four dreams? Not really! Tariq spoke to me only about three of them," said Imelda Griselda also perked up at this and said, "Yes, you told me only about the three nightmares. What is this fourth one about, Ralph?"

Ralph asked Imelda, "Didn't he tell you about another one where his house in Aqlab catches fire and everyone there including his mother and sister perish with him?" Imelda is appalled at this. "No, father! He has never discussed this with me. In fact, until you told me now, I thought he didn't speak about his nightmares to anyone but me. When did he speak to you about them?"

"Oh, many times, dear. He and I had gotten very close after Haroun's death and every time I visited Captain Philip's camp, I would take some time out alone and he has spoken about his nightmares to me too. But, how come he didn't discuss the raging fire? Do you really believe he is dead? Or do you think that the raging fire in his home at Aqlab will be some kind of cathartic effect?"

"You think Tariq is alive and could have made his way back to Aqlab to be with his mother and sister especially now, when the other two nightmares of his seem to have materialized?" asked Imelda. Although Ralph was talking to his daughter, his eyes were fixed on his wife's face. He thought he saw a smirk on her face when Imelda asked about Tariq being alive.

He brushed the thoughts from his head and turned his attention to his daughter and said, "Dear Imelda, I don't know what to think. If he is alive, why has he not come to meet you?"

"Because he wants me to forget him, father?"

"Oh yes, I didn't think of that. Maybe he has really begun to feel the torment of his dreams and wants to put an end to it by going away back to Aqlab. Or he could have thought that if his mother's and sister's lives are in danger, he should be there for them? What do you want to do now, my dear?" asked Ralph, now really concerned for his daughter. She seemed so distraught without Tariq.

"Do you think it might be a good idea to go to Aqlab and speak to Aunt Gabriella and Ayesha?" asked his daughter.

This was what Lady Griselda was waiting for. She was already scheming in her mind as to how to put the ghost of Tariq to sleep in her daughter's mind. She knew that Tariq was dead. There is no way he would have survived the poison from the arrow. But, Imelda was stubborn and didn't want to simply accept that Tariq did, in some way or the other succumb, to his torments. Maybe if she managed to realize this last nightmare of Tariq, she would accept the inevitable. And it would be a great way to get rid of her horrible cousin, Gabriella, whose popularity in Gascoigne and Mordo was soaring now, thanks to her son's noble-hearted healing attitude!

She caught on to what Imelda said and told her husband, "Going to Aqlab would be a great idea. It would give Imelda a change of scene and she would be able to meet her aunt and cousin and find some closure with regard to Tariq."

"You talk as if you know for certain that Tariq is dead, Griselda," said Ralph sternly. His wife realized her folly, "No, I am so sorry, dear Imelda. I did not mean that. Maybe you are right. Tariq could be at Aqlab. Let us go there. And, if God forbid, the rumors about Tariq have reached Aqlab, then his mother and sister will be devastated and they might need our moral support."

So, it was decided that the three of them would get ready and leave for Aqlab the next morning. Griselda was not seen at dinner. When Ralph asked her maids about her, they said that she had some urgent work to be completed before they left tomorrow and had gone out. Now, Ralph's certainty about Griselda's innocence was wavering. What work would she have now which couldn't wait until they returned? And why is she so confident that Tariq's chapter is over? Did she do what Tariq accused her of? He decided to wait and see.

And, anyway, he also had to send word ahead of their departure and let Tariq know that the three of them were on their way to Aqlab. Ralph went in search of his trusted messenger to send word to Tariq and Uncle Esmour.

# *Chapter 9*
## THE FINALE AT AQLAB

T ariq and his grandfather reached Aqlab after two days of riding. The news of his great work had reached Aqlab and everyone was there to welcome the city's favorite son back. Tariq too felt he had come back home and he decided when he stepped across the threshold of his home that nothing would make him leave this place. But, he had to be ready for another sacrifice and he had to get his mother's permission for it.

But even before that, he needed to give time to his mother and grandfather to make up the loss of love for over two decades. The father and daughter hugged and cried in happiness and sorrow. They had celebrated the marriage of Haroun and Gabriella, they had celebrated the birth of Tariq and Ayesha, and they had mourned the death of Haroun; all within a matter of a few minutes of seeing each other. He hadn't seen his mother this happy since the passing of his dad and he was glad that he brought them together.

Just then, the messengers from Uncle Ralph came

and told him what he wanted to hear. Now, he had to speak to his mother and tell her everything and plead for the final sacrifice from her. Fortunately, news of his supposed death hadn't yet reached Aqlab which made it easier for him to relate the entire story since she had left from Captain Philip's Crusade Camp until today. She stared wonderstruck at her son, seeing how much he had grown and matured over the last six months. He reminded her so much of her husband and she was sure that he was looking down from above and feeling exactly the same.

Gabriella readily agreed to do anything that Tariq wanted her to do. She just wanted him to be safe and happy for a long time. She had already warned him about the futility of worrying over nightmares. But, she knew that a lesson learned by yourself is the lesson that will stay longer than if somebody tried to teach you.

The plan was set and now everyone only waited. They didn't have to wait for long. As discussed, all the beds were in his mother's room, Ayesha's, and the servants' rooms appeared to have people sleeping on them but, in truth, everyone was safely staying together in the sturdy tree house built in the dense forest behind their home. The servants had all been told to stay in the university dormitories. The tree house was built for Tariq by Haroun when Tariq was eight. It was spacious and wonderfully strong and could easily keep him, his mother, his sister and his grandfather safe from wild animals and wild men out to get them.

They had fallen asleep waiting for whatever had to happen. Tariq's mother had taken the money and the jewelry with her to the tree house. She was told by her son to forget everything else that was there in the house her husband built for her. Although she knew that something nasty was going to happen to the house, she did not falter. That castle was nothing without Haroun. His love was what made that castle of rock and stone into a beautiful home. She did not think twice when her son suggested his plan.

The four of them had slept through the night completely tired and did not realize it was dawn and a raging fire was burning down their house in the distance. Ayesha screamed in fear. But Tariq consoled her and kept her calm. He looked at his mother and saw that she was shedding tears too but she told him, "Don't worry son. I am not crying because our house is burning down. I am just remembering the good days spent there." Grandfather Esmour was livid with rage that what Tariq said was true. He was hoping, like his nephew, that Lady Griselda would not really have meant to harm her own daughter's love to achieve her ambitions. They all watched as the fire raged and brought the house down slowly and surely.

Soon, Tariq heard some commotion and looked to the right and left and saw six men with hands tied being led by the trained warriors of Aqlab. He had already made arrangements to catch the men who set fire to his house red-handed so that he could use them to reveal Griselda's true intentions.

On the other side of the house, Imelda, Ralph and Griselda were approaching the house. They had traveled all night and as they saw the fire destroying Tariq's home, Imelda screamed and ran towards it thinking that she could at least save her aunt and cousin. But her father held her back and told her, "Don't, my child. It would be futile. It is impossible for anyone to have survived that!" As he pointed to the house, he was staring at his wife and saw a satisfied gleam in her eyes that left him in no doubt that she did what Tariq said she had.

Tariq said he heard the bitterness, the anger, and the hatred when she was talking to him thinking it was Algernon lying in the pit. Tariq had said how proud she sounded that she had ensured she had killed Tariq the same way he thought he would die. Today, Ralph seemed to see the same gleam that must have been in her eyes when she spoke those words to Tariq mistaking him to be Algernon.

They watched helplessly as the fire consumed everything in the house and very soon, there was nothing left except ash and rubble in place of the beautiful castle. Even as it was burning, Ralph could see the startling similarity between this and actual castle at Mordo.

And suddenly, through the hazy smoke and all the mess of the broken and burnt walls, the three of them saw a few people walking towards them. They strained their eyes to see who the people were and to their joy and horror, they realized that the people were Tariq, his mother, his sister, and Grandfather Esmour along with six men whose hands were tied and bound.

Imelda couldn't believe her eyes at the sight of her beloved Tariq and she rushed towards him. He saw the happiness in her eyes and realized what a fool he had been to have run away from such a wonderful girl whose love for him was boundless. But, the most interesting reaction was that of Lady Griselda. She stared shocked and stunned.

"How in the name of the Almighty did you escape the nightshade-tipped arrow that I personally shot at you?"

This question reverberated throughout the neighborhood and no one was more stunned at it than

Lady Griselda herself. She realized that in the moment of utter shock of seeing Tariq alive, she had written her own death sentence. She looked at her husband and saw utter contempt on his face. She turned to Imelda who seemed to have turned to stone when she heard her mother ask that question. She looked at her mother and said, "Mother, what did you say? You shot the arrow at Tariq?"

Griselda, at that moment, realized how she had wasted her entire life running after something without even realizing that the most important thing in her life which was her daughter's love was right there always for her. It was her moment of truth and she realized that it was the worst feeling of desolation and loneliness that she had ever felt. She started to say something. But King Esmour stopped her and said, "Don't try to explain anything, Griselda. These men who were captured as they set fire to the house have already confessed to the crime and they have also confirmed that you were the one to have given them the orders to do it. The men were the same men who prepared the pit ready for Algernon into which Tariq fell."

That is when Griselda realized how Algernon had fooled her and managed to die the changed man he had become. She knew that he must have exchanged clothes to mislead her men. He must have realized she was onto him. She always knew he was the smartest in her team. Oh, how she wished he hadn't undergone a change in his attitude!

The entire truth was revealed to Imelda and Tariq's heart went out to her as he watched her look at her mother with a mixture of pity, sympathy and utter contempt. Tariq knew what it felt to realize that your parent killed for money and power and he knew that his beloved Imelda was going through the same agonizing moments he went through when his father confessed that he was an assassin.

Grandfather Esmour wanted to put Lady Griselda to death for having attempted to kill the heir to the throne of Mordo. But Tariq stopped him. "No, Grandfather Esmour! There cannot be a greater punishment than forgiveness for this lady. She needs to know the pain of having her child hate her. Don't kill her. Just forgive her. I only wanted to make sure that Algernon's legacy lived - that he was indeed a changed man and he died so that I could live. I don't want revenge."

# *Conclusion*

I t was nearly ten years after the day the house of Haroun and Gabriella was burned down. In its place, stood one of the most beautiful hospice care buildings that money could buy then. Haroun had left a lot more money with the ruler of Aqlab and told him to hand it to his son if he died. Tariq used this money to build the hospital and all the sick, wounded and the elderly who needed care were admitted here. There was no discrimination between followers of Islam and Christianity. The Crusades took much longer to end, but in Aqlab, the two communities lived in peace, harmony and happiness.

King Esmour had released an edict making the society of Mordo follow the governing principles of Aqlab. Those who wanted to join the Crusades could go; but within the walls of Mordo, people from both religious communities were welcome and marriages between people from different religions were made legal. There was a lot of opposition from the leaders of both religions as they threatened to tear down Aqlab and Mordo. But the people of both cities stood united and did not allow themselves to be scared of such threats. Eventually, the leaders relented but created another law that no other city in Andalusia, except Aqlab and Mordo, could pass such edicts without the approval of both the religious leaders. For now, Aqlab and Mordo remained happy and safe.

Tariq married Imelda and Ayesha married the second son of the ruling Haisa clan of Mordo. Tariq continued to travel and set up hospices all over in the camps that were part of the Crusades and he was welcomed with open arms by both Moors and Christians alike.

In Aqlab, he built a beautiful but small cottage right next to the hospital building and that was his home. It might have been small as compared to the castle his father built for his mother, but it was wonderful and filled with people he loved from the bottom of his heart.

He shunned all kinds of luxury and wealth and used all the money that his father left towards improving medical conditions at the hospitals. He started a medical school in Aqlab and people from all over Europe came to study there.

Yet, the crusades did not end as fast as he would have liked them to. In fact, he never stopped hearing stories of war and battles and bloodshed. He simply moved on relentlessly doing what he did best; spreading love and compassion and healing as much as he could. His dear wife Imelda accompanied him whenever she could though their two little sons took up a lot of her time.

She had forgiven her mother completely but she couldn't bring herself to speak to her at all. Her father kept visiting them but her mother wouldn't because she knew a murderess was not welcome. Many times, Lady Griselda wished she had been put to death. It would have been easier than the agony of feeling so unloved. When she was nearing her death, she sent word for her daughter to meet her one last time.

Imelda refused to go. Tariq told her, "Didn't you try and convince me that parents' love cannot be replaced when I went through the same emotions with my father? Come, let us go and meet her. Let her feel loved once again. She has suffered enough."

So, she, Tariq and their two sons went to Gascoigne. They reached the castle and went into Lady Griselda's bedroom. Imelda was shocked to see her mother so weak, thin and completely devoid of joy. She ran and hugged her mother who couldn't talk and simply allowed her tears to do the talking. She looked at Tariq who nodded to her kindly and then called her grandsons and clasped them to her bosom. She breathed her last with the joy of having being reunited with her daughter and her family. She died feeling redeemed, happy and at peace.

Imelda thanked Tariq for making her see sense and taking her and the children to see her mother. Yes, everyone had suffered enough. It was time to spread love and peace. After the funeral, the four of them started off in their carriage back to Aqlab watching the beautiful orange glow of the morning sun spread hope and happiness all around.